Navigation Tools to Thrive the Human Experience

2023 Golden Brick Road Publishing House Inc. Trade Paperback Edition

Copyright © 2023 Golden Brick Road Publishing House

www.goldenbrickroad.pub

For more information email: kylee@gbrph.ca

ISBN: 9781989819418

To order additional copies of this book: orders@gbrph.ca

CONTENTS

Disclaimer

If you or someone you know is in immediate crisis or has suicide-related concerns, please call 1-833-456-4566 toll free (In QC: 1-866-277-3553), 24/7 or visit talksuicide.ca.

1-833-456-4566 (24/7)

1-866-277-3553 in Quebec (24/7)

Text to 45645 (4 p.m. – Midnight ET). Text messaging rates apply. French text support is currently unavailable.

Bullying, grief, abuse, anxiety, depression, panic, more...

Kids Help Phone can also support you.

Call 1-800-668-6868 (24/7)

USA: 1-800-273-TALK (8255) to talk to a skilled, trained counselor at a crisis center in your area at any time (National Suicide Prevention Lifeline).

INTRODUCTION

by Kady Romagnuolo

Welcome to the adventurous, enlightening, and sometimes tumultuous journey of the teen years! We all go through them, and the experiences we encounter shape who we become. So, what if we could learn, share, and grow from each other's teen years to cultivate a meaningful future for everyone?

Navigation Tools to Thrive in the Human Experience, A Blueprint for Youth is designed to give youth the tools and resources needed to overcome the challenges faced when growing up. This book is a unique expression of inspiring stories from women of diverse backgrounds and cultures that span multiple generations, providing a wealth of wisdom to explore.

We intentionally designed each chapter with interactive resources to help youth live a fully expressed and abundant life. Here, you will learn how to strengthen relationships, manage emotions, practice self-care, and make positive and healthy decisions. Our younger years are a time of exploration and definition. It's an opportunity to craft an identity that feels congruent to the life that you want to live.

Collectively, we believe that it's time for a change, a big shake-up to acknowledge the real struggles youth face and to validate how strong, creative, and resilient today's youth are.Each author has faced a defining moment in their younger years that carried important messages and unique insights to pass along to the next generation. We wrote from our hearts and shared how even the darkest of nights has a bright light to find. The silver lining in each story is a way out.

You may feel intrigued to flip through the pages to land on a specific story that is meant for you. Or take your time and navigate each one. There's no right or wrong way to read this book. It does not have a beginning or an ending. Each story offers solutions, resources, and options to find a way out of even the hardest challenges. We invite you to dive deeper, explore who you are, and uncover your magic in this world. You get to decide who you will become.

Use these pages to find your most authentic self, connect to your intuition, build confidence, learn how to lead from the heart, and tap into the full potential of your self-expression to thrive.

There is a QR code that you can scan after each chapter to interact with the authors. Learn more, engage in additional conversations, and watch bonus content.

We all know that the teenage years are often among the most difficult and trying times in life. With pressures coming from school, home, and society, it can often be difficult to balance it all. During this time, challenges such as bullying, parents' separation, and low self-esteem can make things even more unbearable. This book is for those teens who feel like they are struggling with these challenges. It offers practical tools and methods to help them cope and develop strategies to maximize their strengths. With this book, we hope to offer guidance, comfort, and reassurance so teens can begin to move forward with joy and resilience.

You will find ways to release anger or sadness, move through depression, develop new habits, navigate bullying, find authenticity, craft your identity, and so much more. Don't wait any longer to take control of your life, the adventure starts now.

Whether you are struggling with anxiety, depression, low self-esteem, or just seeking to grow and develop, this book is here to help you. Through tangible tips at the end of each chapter, you will discover new skills to understand and take charge of your life. This book will empower you to take the steps needed to become the happy and successful person you desire.

CHAPTER ONE

GUESS WHAT? YOU'RE THE HERO.

"It takes one spark to light up your inner Hero."

Naomi N. Ali

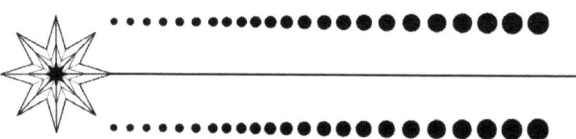

www.nnali.com
www.naominali.com

Fb: naomi.n.ali.leadership.coach
Ig: naomin_ali_leadershipcoach
Youtube: naominali
LinkedIn: naominali-coachandconsultant

Naomi N. Ali

Naomi N. Ali is the CEO of NNALI Consulting, a mission-driven coaching and consulting business championing conscious leadership for the greater good. She is a trusted advisor and Leadership Mindset Coach. As a certified Transformational Coach and Evolved NLP Master Practitioner/Coach, Naomi helps women leaders to overcome career challenges and lead consciously with impact and influence. She combines a progressive corporate career in strategic communications, leadership, and change management to deliver results.

Do you remember your first movie in the theater? My first movie was at a drive-in in my home country of Guyana, South America. The film was *Enter the Dragon*, starring Bruce Lee. It was dope! I remembered the excited feeling that *I* wanted to be the Hero.

A few years later, my family moved to Ottawa, Ontario, Canada. It was a new world of incredible discoveries: stick gum and vending machines, watching the leaves turn colors like sparkly jewels in trees and the wonderment of snow! The most incredible discovery of all was television. My favorite TV show was *Wonder Woman*, starring Linda Carter. I was going to grow up to be Wonder Woman!

I was hooked on action TV shows and movies. I wasn't interested in learning martial arts, boxing, or even fighting; I just loved watching the Hero save the day. Something about the Hero that lit me up.

I certainly didn't look like an action hero; I was a skinny, sporty, seven-year-old with bright eyes and a curious mind, just like most seven-year-olds in my class. Unlike them, though, I was different. I had a Caribbean accent and brown skin, and when you look and sound different from everyone else, all you want to do is blend in or disappear so they don't bully you.

Fast forward. I'm staring at her red face, my hands clenched in a fist and my entire body straight as a board from sheer anger. I had just punched my bully in the face.

Before moving to Canada, I had confidence and bravado. I was the little girl who knew no boundaries. I wanted to be just as adventurous as my older brother; if he could do something, well, so could I! It didn't matter that I was the little sister or a girl. I was brave! There was something in me that wanted to shine. When my family moved to Canada, though, that brave little girl went quiet, and something in me dimmed. For a while.

13

On my first day of school, it was clear I was different, but I didn't *feel* different. That would come later. I remember staring at all the white faces, just as curious about them as they were about me. I remember seeing blonde and even red hair, blue and green eyes, and freckles! Freckles were so cool.

According to my bullies, I was one huge freckle. I had never seen my skin as a color; I didn't know it was brown. It sounds odd, but when you grow up around people like you, it's not something you think of as different. It's just a part of you. And my name! All my life (remember, I was seven at this time), I had been referred to by my middle name (Natasha or Tasha). Suddenly, in Canada, I was referred to by my first name: Naomi. *Who was Naomi?* I remember one kid saying, "Naomi? What kind of name is that?" Well, I thought the same thing!

So now I was different because of my skin color, my name, and my accent. Then there was the fact that I was smart because the school in my home country was advanced. Add "nerd" to the list.

All this was enough for the kids to ridicule, tease, and physically bully me. The name-calling and the physical stuff were hard. Facts. I developed a stutter because they made fun of my Caribbean accent. Now I *felt* different. I just wanted to be invisible, and to be invisible meant not speaking.

Why me? Why don't they like me? Why can't they leave me alone? What's wrong with me? I didn't have the answers, and I don't remember asking.

I don't recall how I made friends during this time. I do remember thinking that not every kid was mean. There were nice kids who didn't care about my color, accent, or name. Not everyone was a bully.

Fast-forward. It's photo day at school. I am wearing hand-me-down clothes from a cousin: my favorite fit and perfect for photo day.

At this point, the bullying had stopped—until a new kid came to school. She was from Australia. She did not like me at all and would throw shade. She couldn't understand how a brown girl was tight and vibing with white friends. Unfortunately, I was learning about racism firsthand. Some kids were racist whether they knew it or not.

On picture day, I had had enough of Miss Australia. We had a showdown, a confrontation in the muddy school yard during recess. Our friends circled us as spectators. She pushed me, and I fell in the mud, dirtying my perfect outfit. I was MAD. I stood up.

Something inside me *sparked*.

I clenched my fist and punched her in the face. She fell back.

My friends gasped in shock. I was in shock! It was the first time I had ever punched someone. When she stood up, her face reddened; she said in her Australian accent, "Oh, I can box, too." And she slapped me. Her slap was weak against my jaw, which was clenched with anger. My entire body was tense with rage. I don't remember what I said, but I didn't move an inch when she slapped me. She walked away with her friends. My friends clapped and cheered me on. Shortly after that incident, she left our school.

I felt strong for standing up for myself. I wasn't scared about the consequences of my actions; I just knew I wasn't going to be pushed around anymore.

This is what you call a defining moment. I learned that I had it in me all along to stand up for myself.

I was the Hero of my movie!

Press pause in the story for an important point: This is about self-defense. If someone is hurting you physically, it's okay to defend yourself if it's safe for you to do so, but then tell adults what happened—immediately.

So that's the story of how I discovered my inner Hero and fought bullying and racism.

I've shared a few important points so far.

Point #1. We all have a spark inside us. It's the call of our inner Hero.

Point #2. Consider why bullies bully.

Point #3. Standing or speaking up changes the behavior.

SPARK YOUR INNER HERO

These key stories from my childhood are imprinted on me: that means they made an impression; they were unforgettable because of what I learned.

I learned that there's a little light or spark inside us. It's called potential or inner strength—or our inner Hero.

You know that feeling of excitement when you're doing a new fun trick on your bike or skateboard, or when you have a great idea, or when something is happening that you don't agree with or like? That's called adrenaline. It may feel like something is moving you to act or speak. It's like a little energy ball inside you. That's the spark.

You may feel an urge to do or say something when you're bullied. You may defend yourself if you think it's safe to do so. You may feel that spark.

OPEN UP

Okay. So notice I'm not mentioning superheroes? That's because superheroes live in the movies. Heroes don't have superpowers. They have a sense of right from wrong and inner strength or courage. Heroes live in real life.

Technically, Batman is not a superhero. (Okay, he's a super-rich hero.) Here's my point. Batman used the bat signal to ask for help from his friends.

Every Hero asks for help at some point. Think about your favorite movie. The Hero is the main character. Did they have people to help them? Yes. And you have people to help you.

You can act on your spark by asking others for help, by opening up and sharing what's happening. This is also important and brave!

If you're bullied in school, online, or in any way, it's okay to ask for help. Speak up and share what's happening with your friends, parents, siblings, and teachers. They will believe you, and they will help you.

Heroes ask for help.

OPEN YOUR MIND

Heroes also have an open mind.

What does that mean? Well, it means seeing something from a different perspective. Have you ever wondered why bullies bully? Why are they salty?

I asked myself these questions. I remember one of my bullies getting picked up at school by his angry dad. It turned out that kid was not in a happy home. He was bullied at home by someone bigger. In either situation, bullying is not okay. But there is a reason why bullies bully.

I never asked my bullies, "What's going on with you? Why are you so mean?"

You don't have to ask them questions either. Instead, just think about why they might choose to behave that way. It is a choice to bully. Why are they choosing to take the time to bully when they could be doing other stuff?

Is it possible they are not happy? Maybe they believe it's the only way to act because that's what they see in their home. Whatever the reason, there is a reason. You may find that you feel sorry for your bullies. Perhaps they need help but they don't know who to ask or how to ask because they haven't found their inner Hero yet.

Maybe you're thinking, *"Why on earth would I think about why a bully is bullying me?"*

Mic drop: Bullying is not about you. It's about them.

This point is super important. When we are bullied, of course we'll take it personally. It's a natural response.

But please try not to.

Remember those questions I asked myself? Maybe you've asked yourself the same ones.

Why me?

Why don't they like me?

Why can't they leave me alone?

What's wrong with me?

WELL, HERE ARE THE ANSWERS!

It's not you. *It's them.*

It's not you. *They don't like themselves.*

It's not you. *They may feel alone in their unhappiness.*

It's not you. *They feel something is wrong inside themselves, so they take it out on others.*

Now it's not on you to figure out the bully or solve all of this by yourself.

The point is, bullying is about the bully.

TBH. It's not about you.

You are awesome. You have a spark. You have a voice.

The moment you feel that spark to speak up or stand up, it will create a change for you. And for the bully.

STAND UP

When you stand up for yourself, you are demonstrating strength. Strength is more than being physically powerful. It's about believing in yourself. That inner spark knows you do not deserve to be bullied.

When you change your behavior or do or say something the bully is not expecting, it interrupts their "plan." It interrupts their pattern of behavior. If they keep doing the same thing and you keep responding the same way, it will not change.

You can't control what the bully says or does.

You only control yourself.

So, feel that spark and either speak up or stand up. Interrupt the pattern. It will surprise them, and when they see that their behavior is not working, it will change. In some cases, it stops.

The critical point here is the moment you stand up for yourself, they will realize something has changed. They will know they do not have control or power over you. Of course, I can't promise that the bullying will stop. Everyone's situation is different. I can promise, though, that the moment you change what you're doing—by walking away, speaking up, standing up, or asking for help and telling others, it will create a change.

Because guess what? You're the Hero of your story.

RISE OF THE HERO

Hey, look in a mirror. That's a Hero!

No mask, no cape, no superpowers.

A Hero knows right from wrong. A Hero has courage and conviction and belief in self.

Psst! That's YOU!

You have that spark inside you to open up and stand up. You have adults who love and care about you; their job is to listen and help you.

Here's the cool part, the part you would never expect but may make a difference. By having an open mind, thinking compassionately about that bully, and speaking up, you may be helping the bully to be a better person.

Another mic drop? Yes.

The Hero saves others, after all.

When we believe in ourselves and understand that we deserve to be treated kindly and respectfully, no one can take that away from us.

The key to standing up against a bully is to be the Hero, not the victim.

You are so much braver than you know.

Roll movie credits.

Ah, but this is not the end.

A preview of the sequel:

You have shiny bright potential! You are meant for so much more. Whatever you put your mind to, you will accomplish. A Hero is also a Leader. You, my friend, are an Emerging Leader.

How to Stand Up Against Bullying: S.O.S

S – Spark your inner Hero

Act on that little spark when something doesn't feel right.

O – Open up. Open-minded.

Open up to adults and tell them about the bullying.

Open your mind is to think compassionately about why the bully is bullying.

S – Stand up

Standing up means interrupting the bully's bad behavior by speaking up, walking away, or self-defense and talking to adults.

CHAPTER TWO

DRESS FOR YOURSELF . . . ?

*"You gave it meaning, so you can change
that meaning, too. Your brain is cool
that way."*

Rebecca Rowe

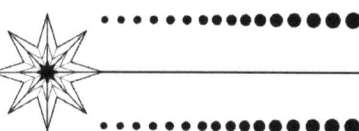

rebeccarowe.ca

Fb: rebeccarowe.ca
Ig: rebeccarowe.ca
Tiktok: rebeccarowe.ca
Youtube: Rebecca Rowe
Goodreads: Rebecca Rowe

Rebecca Rowe

Rebecca Rowe walks through life at six-foot-one, which means that throughout high school, there was nowhere to hide. After years of homeschooling, she walked into a "real" high school where everyone was wearing the cool clothes that never fit her. She had no interest in drawing any sort of attention to herself; in fact, if she could have run home and hid in a closet, she would have! Everyone around her seemed to have cool style, confidence, their lives figured out—everything Rebecca wanted.

Now as a fully trained fashion designer who studied in New York (where she started to learn how to fit in) and Paris (where her six-foot frame stood out like an evergreen in a desert. Forcing her to get comfortable with herself because there was no other choice), Rebecca can look back at her high school self and offer the tools she's learned along the way to help others develop their own personal style. High school Rebecca was as stubborn as grown-up Rebecca is now. The sixteen-year old version of herself would have told her to back off, but without knowing it, that girl is the person adult-Rebecca wakes up every morning to help.

" You're not going to wear *that*, are you?"
Why is it that mothers always have this way of asking questions that make you question everything? I was wearing a pair of black opaque tights with denim shorts over top. IT WAS IN! This was the time when DIY neck-tie skirts were all the rage, and we were "dancing" (read: jumping around to) prissy punk music and wearing tattoo necklaces. They say fashion comes back around every twenty years, and guess what, this is totally back in style now!

Don't judge. I was cool.

The truth was, the look was not all that flattering on my shape. Regardless of whether or not it was totally on-trend. Which it was. It will be my hill to die on, okay!?

Needless to say, when mothers give you THAT LOOK, you either sulk away and completely reimagine your outfit because you want her acceptance and you know somewhere deep down that she's probably right OR you dig your heels in as an act of defiance. Then ten years later, you're sitting in a chair talking to your therapist about the trauma these experiences caused.

I chose to sulk back to my bedroom and change my clothes. When your first-generation Eastern European mother tells you to change after the "You're not going to wear that, are you?" question comes out, you go change.

LET ME TELL YOU. I was AH-noyed. At fifteen years old, I was already six-foot-one (which will later in my life be referred to as five-foot-twelve.), curvy, and looked nothing like any of the girls I saw on TV. I didn't look anything like my friends either, and all I wanted was to be like them.

"Just dress like yourself, Rebecca."

Okay, yeah, yeah, cool. But what does that mean?

We hear this garbage all the time.

"Dress for yourself." But what does that mean? Who am I? And how do clothes "look like me?" How does that make any sense?

"Dress for your body shape." Well. The last time I checked, I was a person, not a piece of fruit, and besides, every internet test gives me a different answer as to what fruit I am. Not great. Those tests are constantly telling me to wear wrap dresses which, I'm sorry, that is just never going to happen.

"You're an autumn." So I'm a fruit and I'm a season? This is not helpful at all.

I'm also a Virgo—does that help with whatever MY sense of style is? Where is the discussion about how clothing can affect your brain, the way you see yourself, the way you show up for yourself and for others, or how the colors you choose can change your mood because of a hormone shift in your brain? How about all the things about clothing that people just don't bother teaching us? If we actually knew the truth, then the fashion industry wouldn't be able to make the billions and billions it makes off us. Actually, the global fashion industry is valued at USD 3 trillion.[1]

You choose your style by first choosing the type of life you want to lead. What is important to you on a YOU level? Do you enjoy sports? Hiking? Reading books? Walking? Being feminine? If it's not what you thought I was going to say, then good. Your style is based on your habits and priorities, not what body type you have.

What are the most important things to you? What do you enjoy? Write whatever comes to mind—there's no right or wrong answer. So if you write, "Tik Tok, Friends, and Money," great. You can't be wrong. If you write, "Reading, Family, Travel," fantastic, that is also correct.

---

1   C. Mair, The Psychology of Fashion (Milton Park, United Kingdom: Routledge, 2018).

1.

2.

3.

As you get older, experience new things, gain weight, lose weight, etc. your style will shift because your priorities and your habits will have changed. You're never locked into any one style, but there may be elements you find that run through your entire life. These elements are a direct reflection of the values you have regarding your personal boundaries.

When I was younger, you couldn't pay me to play sports. I was The Creative in the corner with black eyeliner and pencils in my hair. That's how I chose to represent myself and my interests. I felt like I could connect with others who styled themselves like I did, and they could connect with me for the same reason.

When you develop a friend group with the same set of goals and ambitions you begin flowing with the boundaries that they've set, for life and for how you choose to represent yourself through style. It was in New York City when I first experienced my boundaries being pushed by my friend group.

My first semester of university was in Brooklyn NY and you could feel the excitement radiating out of me. This was my first step to becoming a professional fashion designer. Everyone around me thought it was a bad idea. It was expensive, it was far from home, I had never lived on my own. Telling those around me, "no." was me setting a boundary with them and a very big step for trusting myself.

Remember your first day of school? Meeting new people, excited, nervous, and not entirely sure you were going to make new friends? That was me too. But like you, I made friends. Let me tell you though, when you go to a university for the arts there are A LOT of big personalities. I've never had a loud personality, I'm more of a quiet observer. Don't get me wrong, those quiet ones have personalities, just because I had been looked at for my height my entire life I subconsciously chose clothing that didn't make me stand out. My new friends? They took the opposite approach.

They were all about standing out as the baby-fashionistas they were.

Which is fine, until we would go out and they persuaded me to wear their clothes, which had their values. These pieces, although beautiful, didn't suit my body. Being handed a crop top and my curvy tummy exposed I felt like that fifteen year old being told by my mother to go change.

I wore that top and hated every moment of it. Why? To fit in.

If we go way back to when humans started living together in tribes, they began to adorn their bodies as a way to identify them as part of that specific tribe. We see this across cultures globally.

Charles Darwin wrote that there was no country in the world that did NOT practice tattooing or some other form of permanent body decoration.[2]

Body decoration isn't limited to tattoos; it also includes piercings, jewelry, hair styles, and yes, clothing. Historians look back throughout the ages at figurines, paintings, ancient clothing, shoes, and jewelry to paint a picture about the people who used to be. The earliest evidence of body adornment itself comes from clay figures found in Japan dating back to 5,000 BCE. They depict face painting or engravings to represent tattoo marks.[3]

Please note that this is not permission to go get tattoos if you are underage without your guardian's consent. I'm just giving you the ammo for your argument.

A tattoo, your clothing, the charm around your necklace are all symbols. Symbols only hold meaning when someone gives

2   Olson, A. (2010, April 12). A brief history of tattoos. Wellcome Collection. Retrieved January 12, 2023, from https://wellcomecollection.org/articles/W9m2QxcAAF8AFvE5
3   Olson, A. (2010, April 12). A brief history of tattoos. Wellcome Collection. Retrieved January 12, 2023, from https://wellcomecollection.org/articles/W9m2QxcAAF8AFvE5

them meaning. Those symbols can be personal to you, or they can have a societal meaning. Think about a designer purse for example. Our society recognizes that purse as a symbol of wealth and status. We've come a long way within cultures and society since 5000 BCE, and symbols that used to mean something now mean something else or nothing at all. Look at the Peace Symbol. Even before we get into this, which symbol did you think of? It is going to be different for every person based on your unique experiences. Maybe you thought of the Dove? maybe you thought of two fingers up in a "V" formation? or maybe you thought of the same one I did, the circle with lines in it?

Before it was designed in 1958 by Gerald Holtom, this symbol had never existed. What we now know as the Peace Symbol was originally designed for a protest against nuclear weapons. Holtom used the Semaphore Alphabet (how sailors communicate with flags) to portray the letters "N" and "D", standing for "Nuclear Disarmament." Now we look at this symbol which has been casually printed on a t-shirt and understand its newest meaning: Peace and Justice.[4] When you grabbed that Peace Symbol graphic tee off Shein did you even think of that? Or was it just a cool shirt with a graphic?

Our styles and ways of adorning our bodies may have changed, but the primitive instincts we have about reading body language and symbols have not. We still use physical symbols to distinguish individual status within a group or different groups within a society (a practice still being used today among gangs, schools, militaries, and friend groups).[5] The part of your brain that looks at someone else and says, "You look safe because I understand how you're presenting yourself" is that same part that is prevalent in teens looking to find friends. Safety in numbers, especially in high school and on TikTok.

Groupthink occurs when individual members of a small cohesive group tend to accept a single viewpoint, representing

---

4   J. Prisco, "Three Lines and a Circle: A Brief History of the Peace Symbol," CNN Online, 2019, https://www.cnn.com/style/article/style-origins-peace-symbol/index.html.

5   A. Olson, "A Brief History of Tattoos," BrewMinate, 2019, https://brewminate.com/a-brief-history-of-tattoos/.

a group consensus—regardless of whether some of the group members really believe this viewpoint to be valid or correct. We've seen this a lot in questionable fashion choices made by major players. I'm specifically thinking of Dolce & Gabbana with the "Slave Sandal." Think about how many people saw that prototype, marketing campaign, social media post, and all thought, "Yeah. That's a great name. Won't offend anyone or be taken the wrong way." -Insert groupthink. I know what you're thinking, but groupthink is a big part of what makes a trend so popular. Have you ever found yourself wearing clothes you wouldn't normally wear or that make you a little uncomfortable because all your friends were wearing them? It's the same as that D&G sandal, or me in a crop top.

Has there been a time when you felt like you had to wear something or participate in a trend or conversation that made you uncomfortable?

Share with me . . .

Want an even bigger example of groupthink? One that made history books? The Salem Witch Trials.

It all started with seventeen year-old Elizabeth Hubbard, who began accusing other women of being witches in 1692. The town of Salem experienced mass hysteria, accusing 200 people of witchcraft between February 1692 and March 1693, resulting in twenty executions. The community reached this consensus with practically no evidence[6] (surprise).

"Okay, but Rebecca, what does this have to do with style?"

Trust and your personal set of values. Without them it will be impossible to develop a style that truly represents you.

---

6   Schmidt, "Groupthink Psychology," Encyclopedia Britannica Online, (n.d.), https://www.britannica.com/science/groupthink.

The way you learn to trust yourself is to make yourself little promises and then keep them. Same as you would build trust with someone else. When my father passed away after my first year in New York I didn't go back to school. I started serving tables and living in a daze. I promised myself that I would get back to school and finish what I had started: to become a professional fashion designer.

New York, although I loved it, seemed out of my reach the second time around. That place brought up memories and wounds that I wasn't prepared to fight through. Instead I applied to finish my education in Paris, France. Which is where I learned to trust myself.

Want a challenge? Move to a country where you don't speak the language, you don't know a single person, the city is designed in a way you've never seen, and not a single piece of clothing in a store fits you. Well, except the men's clothing.

Moving to Paris with all of its challenges forced me to really learn to trust myself and to say no. The workload was more challenging, I had less time for friends, I had a roommate that drove me crazy, and all within a world I felt I physically didn't belong. Imagine showering with the shower head at your chest level, or not being able to sit to use the toilet because your knees stuck out the bathroom door.

A lot of boundaries are put in place for us. Things like time boundaries (work or school), physical boundaries (clothing, touch, ect), even monetary boundaries (money and how we think about money). Choosing them for yourself and then defending them? Game changer in the personal trust department.

Don't get me wrong, standing up for your values is not always easy or comfortable. When people challenge your values and beliefs, it can be uncomfortable to tell them, "No." Just remember that "no." is a full sentence and that it will disappoint them, but only for a moment. Whomever you told "no" to, wil move on to someone else who will say yes.

33

Here are a few ways you can politely maintain your boundaries.

1) Practice saying, "no" to small things before moving onto bigger things.

2) Reframe saying "no" to someone as saying "YES" to something you want.

Your body might tell you that you're not feeling all that comfortable by a tightness in your stomach, like you're holding your breath. Or you might argue in your head with what the other person is saying. If you're putting on someone else's clothes, do you pull or tug at the garment? Do you feel exposed? Are you thinking or using the word "SHOULD?"

The first rule when building your personal style: What are your boundaries?

Before thinking about body shape, before you even try on that first pair of jeans, ask yourself what physical boundaries you have and how you want to protect them. Use these questions to help you work through it.

Q. How much skin am I comfortable showing?

Q. If my best friend asked to borrow one of my clothing pieces, would I be okay with that?

Q. How do I want to FEEL in my clothes? (Use words like, "confident," "comfortable," "creative," or "edgy," and then describe what those words mean to you.)

"SHOULD" is the worst word ever when we're talking about your closet. Actually, also your life, but let's start with clothes. Your clothing, your closet is a place of light and happiness. These garments allow you to do everything you want to do in life. They are your armor and your comfort. Don't let things that make you uncomfortable slide their way in there. #boundaries

Your friends may come up to you and say that you "should" be comfortable letting them borrow a garment from your closet. That you "should" be comfortable going out in a mini skirt. If it doesn't make you comfortable, though, then this is where you would set your boundary and say, "No."

1) Understand that your boundaries will be different from anyone else's. What could be extremely important to you may not even register to someone else. [For me, it's my morning routine.]

2) You're not selfish for saying, "No." it may make you uncomfortable, but you're not selfish.

3) Flip it to be on your terms. It could be "NO!" or it could be, "How about like this?"

4) Start with small boundaries and work up as you get more confident.

5) Communicate your boundary clearly. Before you're able to communicate it to someone else, you have to know what what you're wanting to communicate. Do you have your list of what you're willing to do and what you're not?

You can use firm language without being mean or rude. Come at it from a place of kindness and assume positive intent.

I was asked to leave Paris by my partner at the time. He was going through some high-anxiety life events and two weeks before my graduation he asked me to, "come home."

To this day, not holding my boundary of finishing school the way I wanted to finish it, is the biggest regret I have professionally. I was home for six months before he broke up with me and so ended my career in fashion. I mean, how could I leave one of the fashion capitals of the world to come home to Canada and STILL be in fashion?

It was a big lesson to learn: people are inherently selfish.

We are constantly thinking about ourselves, looking at our reflection in the mirror, the phone, the computer, wherever, whenever. We like looking at ourselves. This is how we've learned to thrive for all these years. We protect ourselves. But we can also be mean to ourselves. We can say nasty things to our reflection.

Coming home after my adventures in other countries I beat myself up looking in the mirror. "How could you do this?" "What have you done??" "Great, so we're serving AGAIN!?" My developed style from France faded into comfort clothes. Big sweaters and leggings. About a year of attacking my reflection I chose a new mantra: Be nice to yourself. If you don't take care of yourself, then why would you spend the time adorning yourself the way you want?

This is when I started getting my own tattoos, which are a feature on my arm.

Talking to our reflection and picking apart what we don't like, we're telling ourselves that we're not good enough. That we could be better. That we don't love ourselves. This negative self-talk can OFTEN be brought on by clothing, specifically clothing cost and size.

The clothing industry, or the FASH-UN industry, has different sectors within it. They have children's wear, women's wear, missy (pre-teen), men's wear, activewear, performance wear, and evening wear, all at different price points, made in different factories, and marketed in very different ways. This also goes for beauty products, hair products, and basically anything marketed toward women. The underlying message?

YOU'RE NOT GOOD ENOUGH UNLESS SOMEONE WANTS YOU. This has been the message directed to women for thousands of years. Remember that women were seen as property up until relatively recently in our history and that department stores didn't even install women's bathrooms until the twentieth century.

Think about it. What was the last clothing ad—an actual ad, not an influencer campaign—that you can think of?

If you can't think of any, go to the H&M Instagram account.

We're taught, through nature or nurture, that we're worthy ONCE someone wants us. And even then, the more people who want you, the more valuable you are.

A lot of these messages are not typed out in black and white. I doubt the sales conversion would be there if they did. It's a subtle airbrush here —BE THINNER; a woman with a man's arm wrapped around her waist - HE WANTS ME; a woman running down the streets of Paris in a full ball gown—WHO IS SHE RUNNING FROM/TO? (Okay, that last one is a joke.)

Here are some questions for you to think about:

Q. What is your first thought when you look at yourself in the mirror when you wake up?

Q. What would you like to think?

Q. What's stopping you from getting there?

Q. How can we flip those negatives into a positive?

Realize that you get to control your own brain. You get to think, "I'm the HOTTEST human in the world. My skin is flawless, my body, perfection, and I have a closet that makes Vogue jealous." You could think that. You could believe that.

Look at yourself in the mirror and choose yourself. Choose clothes that make you smile when you put them on, that make you feel comfortable, whatever that looks like for you right now, in this stage of your life. When you are walking around and you catch a glimpse of yourself in the mirror, your first thought is, "Hot damn! I look like I can take over the world." Because you can.

Which leads me to the science.

Enclothed Cognition: The systematic influence that clothes have on the wearer's psychological process.

Embodied Cognition: The theory that we think with our bodies as well as our brains.

Clothes have an effect on how we feel. When we're sick, we want comfort clothing; when we want to feel confident at an event, we wear something else. And there is SCIENCE to back up those feelings!

Researchers from the Kellogg School of Management at Northwestern University led a series of experiments to further understand how our clothing can affect our behavior. In one of their experiments, seventy-four students were chosen at random to wear one of the following: a doctor's white lab coat, a painter's white coat (the same coat), or their own clothes after having seen the doctor's coat. They were then all given a test for sustained attention in which they were asked to examine two similar photos side by side and spot four minor differences and write them down as fast as possible.[7]

Can you guess what happened?

Those who were wearing the perceived doctor's coat found more differences than either of the other two groups. #yeahscience.

Adam. D. Galinsky, who ran the series of experiments, told The New York Times, "Clothing affects how other people perceive us as well as how we think about ourselves." This literally has a name: The White Lab Coat Effect.[8]

So there. If you don't believe me, a fashion designer from Canada, believe the sciencey dude from the United States.

The last thing I want to talk about is the fruit salad in the room. What the bloody hell is an "apple shape" and what does it have to do with who we are and how we dress?! Do "Fashion Rules" even apply to us? Short answer, no. Style is about four fashion theories: balance, proportion, texture, and color.

Balance: Using volume or lack of volume to create shapes on the body.

Proportion: Using clothing to enhance your unique shape.

Texture: The feel that your clothes have both within your look and on your shape.

Color: The colors you choose to enhance your natural beauty.

---

7   S. Blakeslee, "Mind Games: Sometimes a White Coat Isn't Just a White Coat," New York Times Online, 2012, https://www.nytimes.com/2012/04/03/science/clothes-and-self-perception.html.

8   Ibid.

No fruit. No boxes. No math. . . . Okay, maybe some math. Balance and proportion are math.

What is proportion in fashion? Simply defined, it is the relationship between two components. Within fashion and style, we can use proportion to manipulate the eye, play with shape, and highlight the areas of your body that you love. #MATH

Remember the tights & shorts combo where my mum told me to go change? The problem with the outfit was that the proportions and shape of the clothing were unflattering to the proportions and shape of my body. Had the shorts been longer—it is always the clothes and never your body—and a little bit wider around the thigh, that outfit would have worked.

The easiest way to play with style is by playing with proportion and volume. Remember that your body is the base that you're building on top of. To build your style, you want to start by identifying the areas of your body you love.

I love my . . . (Do it! Say it out loud: I LOOOOOVE MY . . .)

1.

2.

3.

Did you go to the mirror and say what you loved?? - I know that may not have been super comfortable, but you did it!

What!? You didn't? Go do that and come back.

Use clothes to point arrows to those areas. If you love your face, wear color and collars, all up near your face.

If you like how small your waist is, use volume on the top and the bottom to really bring that attention to your waist. You can also do this by making a "line" with a color break, belt, or tie at your waist.

Have fun, experiment with clothing, and make sure it fits your body, your personality, and your lifestyle. This means that if you love to run, then have running shoes in your closet—even if the "cool kids" don't.

Remember when your mother said, "Dress like you"? If you don't know who you are, you can't have a "personal style." Clothing is a physical representation of your HABITS, PRIORITIES, and LIFESTYLE. First define what those elements are and then visualize them to give you exactly what you're looking for: Confidence.

Clothing can make you feel invincible, it can manufacture confidence, and it can also make you feel comforted and remind you of special occasions.

But clothing can also make you feel like an imposter, like you're trying too hard to be someone you're not. Clothing only means what we allow it to mean. That dress you bought that you don't fit in anymore—what does that mean to you? Because the dress is just a piece of cloth that has been sewn into a shape.

You give it meaning, so you can change that meaning, too. Your brain is cool that way.

HOW TO: VISUALIZE CONFIDENCE

First things first, my dude: confidence is a feeling, not a personality trait. Which means you don't feel it all the time. In fact, you feel confident in specific clothing actions, situations, etc. The easiest way to feel confidence is to be comfortable, which takes practice. But with practice, you can always feel comfortable with yourself, if not with your situation.

When you think about yourself, specifically your appearance, what comes to mind? Don't overthink it; just write what comes to mind, "good" or "bad."

1)
2)
3)
4)
5)

Perfect. Now what do you believe about those things you just wrote down?

1) Belief:
2) Belief:
3) Belief:
4) Belief:
5) Belief:

Your identity is the collection of your experiences, which make up your beliefs about yourself, which make you feel things, which make you behave a certain way, which gets you results (experiences), which leads back to the beginning of the cycle.

41

Now write down how you want to think about yourself, specifically about your appearance.

1)

2)

3)

4)

5)

What does that look like? Pull up photos from Pinterest, write a description, whatever makes it easier for you to visualize those characteristics.

Finally let's put them together with how you see your (current) lifestyle, vibe, and body shape.

Vibe:

Lifestyle:

Body:

Which eleme nts fit into your existing habits? Which habits are you willing to change to be able to pull in some confidence factors?

Need more help? Use this QR code for a full video.

CHAPTER THREE

FREEDOM FROM SELF-JUDGMENT

"Embracing our differences and uniqueness helps us own our inner brilliance."

Marisa Brona O'Brien

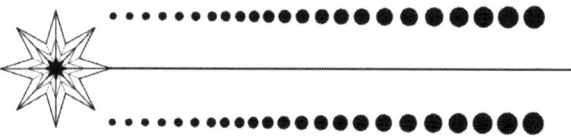

www.marisaobrien.com

Fb: parentbreakthrough
Ig: parentbreakthrough
Tiktok: marisaobriencoaching
Youtube: Marisa O'Brien

Marisa Brona O'Brien

Marisa Brona O'Brien is a Master Practitioner of Evolved Neuro-Linguistic Programming and has a Bachelor of Science. She is certified in multiple modalities, including Quantum Change Process™, Quantum Goal Setting™, hypnosis, and Reiki and is a trauma-aware transformational coach. Marisa is passionate about helping parents gain a more in-depth understanding of themselves to become aligned with who they are and who their children are, so they can feel good in their mind and body.

Marisa uses specialized tools to discover the root cause of what holds us back from owning our innate brilliance and living the life we desire. She helps parents expand their perspective to gain a more profound understanding of their child's experience, develop meaningful connections, embrace imperfection, and re-define themselves so they can lead the way for their families. Her clients overcome guilt, frustration, and exhaustion while enjoying more balance and energy to truly enjoy their parenting experience; they also learn how to support their children in developing healthy self-confidence, self-acceptance, and unconditional love so they too, can embrace who they are and live a joyful and vibrant life.

I believe we are all on this planet for a reason, and part of that is to share our unique talents and gifts. Growing up, it can be so easy to get sucked into trying to fit ourselves into made-up illusions of what we think perfection looks like or how we "should" be. Feelings of being not good enough, anxiousness, and self-doubt creep in. We start to question our capabilities. We separate from our true self. We try to create as much distance as possible from our perceived flaws and unattractive qualities, keeping them hidden, forming judgment around ourselves and others who have these qualities. Even worse, we shame ourselves for having them.

I have found in my work that it is these exact qualities that lead us to our brightness, the most brilliant abilities we have within. Say what!?! Yeah, take a mind-blowing moment.

What we don't like about ourselves leads us to our greatness. In our shadows lies a roadmap to our strength. To find this buried treasure, we need to get curious about the most hated parts of ourselves, unmask them, and work toward accepting all parts of ourselves so we can tap into our hidden strengths and learn to love ourselves unconditionally—misfit quirks and all.

PAINFULLY SHY

I was a bubbly, happy child, in awe of the world around me. Being goofy was part of my daily life. I would dress in silly outfits, make up new lyrics to songs, and of course tease my little brother. I loved to be funny, yet I was also painfully shy with kids I didn't know and incredibly sensitive. I hid behind my mom's back when anyone new was introduced, my blood pumping so hard that the surrounding voices became a blur. I was painfully shy, and meeting new people and speaking out in a group seemed impossible. As I went through elementary school and middle school, I tried to push through my shy, sensitive nature, but it still had such power over me.

As I moved into my 'tween years, I also started to become self-conscious about my goofy side. I began to notice social "norms" around me and felt like a misfit. I took on certain beliefs: namely, that girls needed to be proper yet sexy, smart yet ditzy, funny but not too funny. Anxious that my silly, timid personality wouldn't fit that mold, I slowly started masking my personality and stifling my own voice even more to avoid conflict and rejection. I wanted to belong.

I'm highly sensitive, meaning I felt everything. And teenager emotions are intense. I didn't realize that most of what I was feeling wasn't even mine. It was like I was an emotional punching bag for those around me struggling with anger, frustration, and feeling not good enough. I soaked it all in like a sponge, I had no idea how not to take it all on or how not to get upset. I believed that they were all my feelings and that I was just overly sensitive and emotional. Not fun.

THE REBELLION OF "NOT ME"

I thought I needed to be tougher and less sensitive. More attractive and less goofy. More outgoing and less shy. I was on a mission to figure out how to be a different me.

As I continued to separate from who I was and become who I thought I needed to be, I joined the high school cheerleading team. I would learn to fit in there, be popular and outgoing, start figuring out how to be "not me" and put on a new skin. Yet when I started to become more "normal" (or what I perceived as normal at the time), I started to become judgmental of anything "normal."

Enter a paradox! I no longer wanted to be seen as goofy, shy, or sensitive, yet I also wanted to be anything but basic. I started testing boundaries. I rebelled against the word "normal" and found other ways to show my uniqueness—ways that didn't result in conflict, of course, because I was still terrified to speak up for myself and or to be questioned. Gulp! I started creating my own clothes and personal style and embracing music that was anything but mainstream. Yet I continued to keep my true sensitivities and shyness hidden from most, keeping my inner voice quiet and the projection of who I wanted to be loud. I was masking.

We mask the very thing that makes us special so we can "fit in." Masking becomes a survival lifestyle, a way to camouflage our true self and create a rendition of behaviors that are seen as more socially acceptable. Masking is especially common for neurodivergent individuals. Neurodivergence is the concept that humans vary in their mental or neurological function; while we all have strengths and weaknesses, neurodivergent people have different talents and challenges from what is considered normal. Neurodivergence is associated with diagnoses such as ASD (Autism Spectrum Disorder), ADHD (Attention Deficit Hyperactivity Disorder), and Anxiety Disorder.

I personally reject the word "disorder"; I find the word to be demeaning when used to describe the intricacies of how someone functions and processes things. Labels can lead us to a better understanding of ourselves; however, they can also pose challenges, especially when they end with a word like "disorder." Ew! Interestingly, neurodivergent people are often processing more information instead of less, but the label "disorder" (at least, to me) implies there is something wrong and "less-than." The truth is, though, there is so much right that is happening—it's an evolution of neurology and additional abilities we have not yet begun to use to our fullest potential. I think labels can give us some answers and a deeper understanding of ourselves and those around us, but they ultimately do not define who we are or what we are capable of.

Do the labels you give yourself have a positive or negative connotation for you? If there is a negative implication, how can you reframe it to shed light on your fierce side instead of the side you don't like?

Cheering helped me mask, but it also taught me to use my voice and escape my comfort zone, at least for moments. They call it a comfort zone, but for me, it seemed more like an invisible prison cell filled with self-doubt and questioning thoughts that I couldn't even follow half the time. The comfort zone is anything but comfortable—it's confining.

Over time, "not me" started to become fun! Testing boundaries, pushing limits, getting noticed for wacky outfits and crazy hairstyles. Self-expression felt good. In being "not me," I was actually tapping into things that I never knew about myself.

As I continued to push out of my self-imposed prison, the less difficult it became. Don't get me wrong: I still felt like I wanted to barf half the time before a performance or when speaking up for myself, but I had a squad around me now, so I knew I wasn't alone.

Speaking up on my own without the familiar faces was still a big problem, though. That painfully shy girl inside of me would shrink down to what felt like half my size. All of my thoughts would blur, I would feel stupid, and I would people-please and politely agree instead of standing up for myself. In fact, I didn't speak up even when something didn't seem right to me. I stayed quiet and didn't speak my truth. Any form of conflict was swept under the rug.

Each time I avoided confrontation, I became a little more confused about who I was. Was I still that shy girl, or was I a fearless teen? I was stuck. Trapped in my own self-judgment. Part of me felt amazing, fearless, and unique just the way I was, while the other part felt completely inadequate, terrified, and shameful to show who I really was.

IN OUR SHADOWS WE FIND OUR STRENGTH

Who am I? How do I accept or overcome what I don't like about myself? How can I find my inner confidence? How do I become who I want to be?

One thing I have found to be true is that every challenge I face leads me to a deeper understanding of myself. The more I learn about the real me, the more clarity I have. As long as I can stay in a place of curiosity and avoid blaming myself and others, I become more clear and confident with who I am.

When I was younger, I had no idea that my sensitivity was also a strength. You know, the sensitivity I basically spent all my time trying to mask. I mean, how could taking on others' negative emotions like a sponge absorbing water be a good thing? How could crying whenever I was questioned or confronted be an asset?

I was dumbfounded as to how the things I desperately tried to hide and squash from my life could be inherent strengths. It didn't make rational sense to me, but I was open to exploring. If you're open to a little adventure yourself, join me in exploring your hidden truths on a journey to find your inner strength and ultimately self-acceptance.

Play along and list the parts of yourself you try to hide:
What don't you like about them?
What do they do for you?

You may be wondering how my sensitivity helped me. When I dug in, I found that it allowed me to connect with people and tune into their emotions. I could easily put myself in other people's shoes and experience things as if I was them. I discovered I am a highly sensitive person (HSP): someone who has developed a deeper central nervous system sensitivity to physical, emotional, environmental, or social stimuli.

So putting myself in somebody else's shoes and allowing them to unburden themselves and feel better was supportive, right? Well, for them, it was. I, on the other hand, was absorbing it like a sponge getting heavier and heavier with water. Ugh. So now what?

Now get curious!
What is the good in it?
What can you learn from it?
How does it benefit you?
What change needs to be made?

The choice to look at my sensitivity as a strength instead of a weakness was a turning point for me. Some use the label "empath," while others resonate more with HSP. Either way, like I said before, labels can help us gain a deeper understanding of ourselves and know we are not alone. Aligning with being an empath and opening up to the possibility that my sensitivity was a gift shifted my perspective. I could choose to no longer look at my sensitivity as a detriment to my life and instead see it as one of my best qualities. I had a beautiful ability to be more in tune to others. However, I also learned that I couldn't let that label totally define me. Being a sponge sucked! I needed to figure out how to set healthy boundaries.

TAPPING INTO OUR INNATE BRILLIANCE

I find self-discovery to be incredibly empowering. It's a way to tap into who we are and who we want to be. Grab a pen and paper and answer the following questions:

Who do I admire?
Who do I want to be more like?
In what ways am I like them already?

The interesting thing is we cannot see what is not within us. If there is something we love about someone else, we also have that strength ourselves or hibernating within us. This is also true for people who bother us. When there is something that triggers us, it gives us a glimpse into a part of ourselves we dislike or a past experience or trauma we still need to heal. So now ask yourself:

Who irritates me?
What specifically about them irritates me?
What does that have to do with me?

Writing down what we love and what we try to hide opens up the door for self-discovery. Digging into what our triggers have to do with us is an opportunity to gain perspective on what we need to work on or do for ourselves.

I needed to learn how to manage my energy and protect my emotions while still being able to connect to others; I needed shielding boundaries to deflect others' negative energy back to them instead of soaking it all in, and boundaries to speak up for my own needs. I unfortunately didn't learn how to do this until way after I graduated from university but if I could go back in time and change anything, shielding and boundaries would be it.

Expressing and holding boundaries is a life skill that many struggle with. First we need to know what boundaries we need to set in our life. What is okay and what is not and with whom? Take a moment and ask yourself what you need.Sometimes a boundary isn't about speaking at all but rather walking away from what doesn't align with you.

Knowing what we don't need and what we do need gives us clarity. Sometimes to protect those needs, we have to push outside our comfort zone one step at a time. When we do, we build self-trust. Oh, what I would give to time travel back to my twelve-year-old self and teach her boundaries? Our boundaries are not what others say they should be—they are unique to us. They are what we are willing to allow in and what we are not, and then using our voice to express what is or is not okay.

Lastly, boundaries are making choices to support our needs. Nobody, and I mean nobody, knows you better than you know yourself. If someone says otherwise, they can't yet comprehend an experience so different from their own.

For me, tapping into my inner self and embracing who I was (and who I am now at this moment) allowed me the freedom to express my needs and set appropriate boundaries. If we all embraced our uniqueness, silliness, and quirks, there would be more acceptance and less of a divide. I invite you to own your uniqueness, as I am embracing mine. We can all rise together.

FREEDOM FROM JUDGMENT

When we try to keep ourselves boxed up inside this expectation of perfection and fitting in, we lose our connectivity to who we are. When we embrace ourselves and all the imperfections and mistakes we've made, any shame and judgments attached to them are released. We are free from our own self-imposed shackles, and we no longer let others' judgment define us. We now know their judgments are just a part of them that they do not like nor accept inside themselves.

Curiosity is the beginning of self-discovery that leads to freedom from judgment. It is a normal human response to judge. Awareness comes when we allow ourselves to get curious. Insight into when and why something is happening helps us to gain a deeper understanding of ourselves.

When we judge others, that is our signal to look within. Find the why behind the judgment to break the cycle. Warning: the insight that comes out may be perceived as a flaw. This is natural. Embrace it anyway! There are two sides to every coin and even if it's something you don't like about yourself, on the opposite side lies one of your greatest strengths. It's not about hiding from our weaknesses or flaws but rather owning them and our strengths at the same time.

At the same time, what we imagine others think about us is our own inner self-critic talking, often resulting in self-sabotage. We make up these stories about what others are thinking about us when in reality, it is our own thoughts that are lifting us up or tearing us down. Our projection of what others think about us rules our self-confidence.

What is it that you believe about yourself?
What do you think others are thinking?
Are these supportive or unsupportive beliefs?

If they are unsupportive, how can you change that story in your mind to support you in becoming who you want to be?

What is the new belief you would like to have?

Releasing our own self-judgment frees us and allows us to shine as we were meant to. As we do, it unknowingly gives permission to those around us to also release their self-judgment. We rise together.

The possibilities for you are limitless. Use who you want to be and how you wish to feel as a catalyst to spark supportive self-talk. This will ultimately give you the power over your life and the freedom of choosing your journey. You are the creator and expert of your own experience.

"You can't go back and change the beginning, but you can start where you are and change the ending."

–C.S. Lewis

WE ARE ALL MEANT TO SHINE

Our most powerful inner strength comes from the most difficult challenges we have overcome. Not one human on the planet thinks and feels the same way, and that is what makes all of us special. We can share similarities and learn from our differences.

"Neurodiversity describes the idea that people experience and interact with the world around them in many different ways; there is no one 'right' way of thinking, learning, and behaving, and differences are not viewed as deficits."[1] There are many ways of doing things that are outside our own individual ways of thinking because we all have different experiences and thinking patterns. This is a beautiful thing—it proves that the way we are thinking could be right at the same time that someone with an opposite viewpoint is also right. A paradox of two truths. This knowledge can lead to great collaboration and acceptance of others and ourselves.

Accepting who we are and owning our uniqueness comes from facing our dislikes about ourselves head-on. I wanted to

---

1   Nicole Baumer and Julie Frueh, "What is Neurodiversity?," Harvard Health Publishing, November 23, 2021, https://www.health.harvard.edu/blog/what-is-neurodiversity-202111232645.

separate myself and be unique, yet I also wanted to belong. I have learned to embrace multiple truths about myself and to love and accept both who I want to be and as I am right now, strengths and weaknesses alike. Ultimately, I've discovered that I can belong and be unique at the same time as long as I am not sacrificing my authentic self to fit in.

One of my favorite quotes is by author Marianne Williamson: "Our deepest fear is not that we are inadequate. Our deepest fear is that we are powerful beyond measure. It is our Light, not our Darkness, that most frightens us. We ask ourselves, who am I to be brilliant, gorgeous, talented, fabulous? Actually, who are you not to be? You are a child of God, your playing small does not serve the world. There is nothing enlightening about shrinking so that other people won't feel insecure around you. We are all meant to shine, as children do. We were born to make manifest the glory of God that is within us. It's not just in some of us; it's in everyone. And as we let our own light shine, we unconsciously give other people permission to do the same. As we are liberated from our own fear, our presence automatically liberates others."[2]

I believe that embracing our differences and our own uniqueness helps us to evolve and accept one another. We judge what we do not know, when we should be curious instead so we can learn and grow together. What we change within ourselves will have a ripple effect across space and time for generations to come.

You are a unique gift to the world and humanity. Your voice matters. You matter. What you tell yourself matters. You are more than enough and have been since the moment you came into this world. My wish is for you to honor and love yourself as you are now.

Permission to be perfectly imperfect!

Yours truly,

Marisa

---

2   Marianne Williamson, 1992, Return to Love: A Reflection on the Principles of a Course in Miracles. (New York, NY: Harper Collins).

How to Uncover Your Shadows and Strengths:

Play along and list the parts of yourself you try to hide:

- What don't you like about those parts?

Now, get curious and answer these questions with the first response that pops into your mind! What is the good in it?

- What can I learn from it?
- How does it benefit me?
- What change can I make?

Next, discover your shadows:

- Who irritates me?
- What specifically about them irritates me?
- What does that have to do with me?

Lastly, uncover your hidden strengths:

- Who do I admire or want to be like?
- What is it specifically that I like about that person?
- In what ways am I like them already?

The interesting thing is we cannot see what is not within us. If there is something we love about someone else, we also have that strength ourselves or hibernating within us. This is also true for people who bother us. When there is something that triggers us, it gives us a glimpse into a part of ourselves we dislike or a past experience or trauma we still need to heal. On the flip side of your shadow lies your greatest strength. So what is the opposite of your shadow?

Now create a new belief you would like to have. If you're unsure, try "I love and approve of myself as I am." Repeat your new mantra daily.

CHAPTER FOUR

MAKE YOUR OWN MAGIC!

*"You have the power to change anything
you want in your life. You are magic!"*

Kady Romagnuolo

www.coachkady.com

Fb: kady.romagnuolo
Ig: kady.romagnuolo
Tiktok: coachkady

Kady Romagnuolo

Kady Romagnuolo is a business coach for heart-led entrepreneurs, top-performing real estate broker, and professional who helps entrepreneurs get aligned, break through their limits, and realize more profits by understanding the natural seasons of sales. She is a multiple best-selling and award-winning author, as well as a podcast host and an international speaker on the world tour for Think and Grow Rich.

As a certified NLP (Neuro Linguistic Programming) Master Practitioner, Kady takes a unique approach that blends brain science with the power of natural moon cycles to create transformational sales results that feel like magic!

She is the founder of Moonlogic® Magic School, the first intuitive online portal to help transform heart-led businesses from passion project to six- or seven-figure empire.

I hated being different. I was great at pretending I was a cool kid, like nothing bothered me, but on the inside, every day was hard. My dad was super strict, and didn't allow me to do things that seemed normal for other kids. I couldn't listen to secular music; in my household, if someone wasn't singing about God or something religious, it was bad or evil. I never wanted to have friends over because I was afraid my dad would have an angry outburst or make me feel stupid in front of them. I felt like I couldn't ever do anything right, so I learned to be the quiet, shy kid in the corner, to smile and nod in public because it was too scary to disagree with someone.

At heart, I was a fun little girl with so much spirit. My favorite thing to do was watch magic shows: these grand television productions with huge theaters packed with an audience ready to watch the world's best magicians perform incredible tricks. In my mind, there was no way magic wasn't real. I couldn't figure out how these could just be tricks to entertain the audience. On these nights, I could get lost in the show and escape from my reality.

I used to imagine that one day, I would become a famous magician and I would practice all of my magic tricks for whoever would watch. It was the most exhilarating time in my life: believing I could be anything.

When I was thirteen, I heard a loud thump at my door.

"Get your stuff; we're leaving!" my mom said in a stern but shaky voice. I could see she was afraid by the look on her face and was trying to get me to hurry so we could leave the house. This wasn't unusual. My parents would fight, everything in the house would get smashed, and we would frantically leave to escape. After a while, a frantic bang on my door became expected, almost normal instead of scary.

I was wearing white track pants you could see through and polka-dotted underwear. I had been just hanging out in my room, thinking I would go to sleep soon; instead my whole life changed in that moment. We never went back, and I had to start high school living out of a bag at the home of a relative with not much more to wear than my white track pants you could see my underwear through.

I had to try so hard to have friends. No one seemed to really notice me. It wasn't that I was picked on; it was more that I was completely invisible much of the time. Not the kind of magic I had hoped for. After so many years of being the quiet, shy girl so that I didn't ruffle any feathers at home, I had become the girl who faded into the back corner, the girl nobody waited for at lunch. If I didn't rush to my locker to find someone to eat with and pretend like I was part of a group, laughing and joking along to be accepted, suddenly I would find myself all alone in the hallway, feeling like the biggest loser because I had no friends.

Feeling left behind and like no one cares if you're there or not is excruciating. All I wanted was for someone to wait for me, to notice me, to ask me if I wanted to join them. It felt so embarrassing, so instead of trying to make friends, I got really good at learning how to avoid people and pretending that everything was okay and that I didn't care.

When I felt lonely, I didn't tell anyone; instead I found somewhere I could be alone and sad where nobody could see.

When I felt like there were too many people around and I didn't know what to say or how to fit in, I would pretend to be in a hurry to get somewhere, like I didn't have time for them. Then I'd find somewhere nobody could see me to wait all on my own until the crowd was gone.

I was fabulous at being fake but in reality, I had so much social anxiety that I just didn't know how to be me. I didn't know how to let others see me for the fun, magic-loving little girl who wanted to dress in bright colors and tell cheesy jokes.

But I like to think that there was always someone or something looking out for me. (I think you have something special looking out for you, too! That's how you found this book—I wrote this message just for you, hoping you would find it.) I always had a little voice inside, even when I tried to ignore it, helping me become the magician I always wanted to be.

Things felt really hopeless at times, and I thought I would never be accepted or truly loved or get to have a job that was fun and made lots of money. Most of the people I grew up around had to work really tough jobs for not very much money and were too tired to have fun, wear bright colors, or watch magic shows. But I would daydream about being a magician even though it felt like it would never really come true, and I was able to get lost in that feeling, knowing somehow my life was going to turn out well. I didn't know how, and at times it felt impossible that I would ever get out of my rough neighborhood, but I just kept daydreaming.

Do you ever imagine that you are somewhere else, doing something that makes you really happy? I didn't know it back then, but this is actually a really powerful thing to do. When you daydream about something that makes you feel good, it activates something inside of you that then finds ways for what you're dreaming about to come true. There's some interesting science (and really boring statistics) that explain this phenomenon, but basically your mind is so powerful that it doesn't really know whether you are pretending something is real or whether you are experiencing it in real life. And there's one secret ingredient that I learned later on in life that you can use to create exactly the life you want—almost like magic! I've used this trick to become super successful at exactly the dream job I always wanted: a magician!

Thoughts can change your life in really magical ways if you know how to use them. The key to having good things start to happen quickly is connected to how you feel when you are imagining something in your mind. Your feelings are the secret code that shows you exactly how to have what you want.

When I was daydreaming about being a magician, it was thrilling. I would think about being on stage in a sparkly dress, imagining I was really there looking out to the audience, feeling what it would be like if I could really perform magic. It was exciting; it was fun, and it always made me feel good. Even if just for a minute.

Remember how I said there are some boring statistics that show how this really works? I started researching it as an adult, and it turns out when you visualize yourself doing something and really imagining that you're actually doing it and feeling what it would be like to really be there, your mind decides that you have actually really done the thing you're imagining and creates new skills. Poof—just like magic. Turns out, I was practicing without ever being on stage. You're getting what's called muscle memory, when you feel like you have a natural ability to do something a lot more easily, as if you practiced for hours. And the better you feel while you're imagining yourself doing what you really want to do, the faster this works!

When I grew up, I realized the things I loved as a little girl were clues to who I would become later in life. I loved magic for a reason; it was fun to tell people about all the weird, cool tricks I learned. It turns out that the things I thought were weird or maybe different from others actually made me interesting and were the secret ingredient that later helped me be successful.

I now get to talk about magic on stage just like I imagined all those years ago, and it feels just like it did when I was pretending. The moment I step on stage, I activate that little part of my brain that feels like I've done this before. It helps me feel confident and ready to do anything. That's what muscle memory is: when you feel like you've done something before, so it feels easy. It's like riding a bike. Once you've learned how, you just ride without thinking about how to pedal or balance.

Because of this simple little trick I didn't know I was using, I grew up to open a successful magic school where I teach others how it's okay to be weird, different, or not fit in. How those are actually the things that make you special. That if something brings you joy or creates happy thoughts, it's good to explore it.

So, would you like to learn how you can do this, too, and create your own magic?

Awesome! I had a feeling you would. First things first: what's one thing you would like to have happen in your life right now? If you could wake up tomorrow and do anything differently, what would you want to experience? If you could see and change your future, what kind of magic would you create? (Psssssst—there are no wrong answers here! You can literally be, do, or have anything in the world.) Go ahead, write it down here so you remember it later:

Great job! I'm excited for you as I'm writing this because I can already tell that your words are powerful and you are super unique!

Next, I'm curious to know more about you, since you now know a bit about me. Imagine that these pages are able to travel through time back to me like an instant teleportation device that creates a line of communication between us. It feels kinda magical to know that we are connected in some way, doesn't it? Here we go—a few questions for you:

What's one thing you want me to know about you?

Do you have any challenges you would like to find solutions for? (I'm going to imagine now that you find the perfect solution that feels really good for this exact problem, so only write something that you want to find answers for. Remember, the mind is really powerful so as soon as you do this, don't be surprised if some really cool, great things happen for you:

Okay, are you ready to learn how you can use your powerful mind to create your own magic and change your future? Check out the next page. You can even rip that page out and carry it with you as a reminder for anytime you are feeling lonely, scared, worried, or frustrated. You have the power to change anything you want in your life. You are magic!

How to Magically Change Your Future

1) Think about the future you want to create for yourself, the one you wrote on the page before.

2) Imagine you are really there, like you're in a movie.

3) Notice every detail. Is there anyone with you? What are you doing in this moment?

4) Imagine what it feels like. Is it fun, calming, warm, happy, exciting? You get to choose.

5) Now close your eyes and practice being there as often as you can. Remember to really imagine feeling fabulous as you do this (that is the secret code).

Would it be fun to have someone to guide you through this practice? I would love to help because I know how powerful this is. Scan this little code to watch the video, and we can do this together! See you there.

CHAPTER FIVE

SURVIVING THE SEVENTH GRADE

"It is possible to put the pain of childhood trauma behind you and create a life full of beautiful experiences."

Leslie Anne Hook

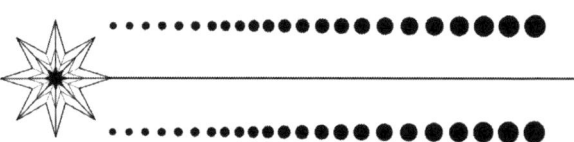

www.urbanrunaway.ca

Fb: urbanrunaway

Leslie Anne Hook

Leslie Anne Hook is a student of human rights and social justice at Carleton University in Ottawa, Ontario. She is a child protection activist who researches childhood victimization and cases of non-familial abuse within institutional settings. Her research focuses on safety audits of youth-serving organizations and advocating for the implementation of mandatory sexual abuse prevention training for all adults working with children in a community setting.

A survivor of complex childhood trauma, Leslie Anne advocates on behalf of survivors across Canada and is a dedicated facilitator of Trauma Shift, a community-led support group connecting individuals who have walked a similar path. Leslie founded Urban Runaway Inc., a Canadian impact agency on a mission to unite a network of safe spaces and organizations that work together to provide skill-building programs and personal development opportunities for youth. Barrier-free education also is important to Leslie Anne, and she supports alternative learning pathways for youth who struggle in a traditional school setting and for mature students requiring guidance reintegrating into the formal learning environment.

The mother of two children, Leslie Anne spends her spare time embracing a rural lifestyle in the Ottawa Valley, enjoying outdoor activities with her family and participating in community social events.

When I was a little girl, my grandmother told me that everyone is born with a white light inside of them, a light that glows during our greatest time of need and acts as a compass for our entire life.

It is remarkable how quickly it all happened. An unexpected series of devastating events in middle school left me in a life-or-death battle to survive the seventh grade. This is my teenage survival story, a cautionary tale for youth and the adults who care for them. A glimpse into the dysfunctional middle school experience of a disempowered adolescence, and how I found my voice as a young adult to speak out against child abuse.

It has been over twenty-five years since I last stepped foot into my childhood middle school, but the smell of freshly painted walls and newly inflated basketballs still lingers. The desks had never been used, the playground never explored. There was a calm before the storm as the summer ended and I entered my seventh-grade year. Life would never be the same for our suburban family.

A newly constructed school, the building was very modern, with a state-of-the-art computer lab and an amazing curb appeal that included modern playground features and two life-sized pencils holding up a new school sign. It created the perfect backdrop for my first-day-of school photos. It was an exciting time to be a kid, and I thought it was pretty darn cool to be the first class of grade six students to have ever graduated from the new school with the impressive blue roof. Little did I know, my grade six graduation would be the last academic milestone celebrated in my childhood.

Unsafe Environments for Youth

In Canada, most schools have at least one. We even have a special name for them: a quiet room. On paper, the benefits of a quiet room seem helpful. A special room designed to function as a safe space for children who require a sensory controlled environment so they can regain composure after an outburst and quickly reintegrate back into the classroom.

But what happens when these intended rooms are misused and create an unsafe environment?

I was twelve years old when first introduced to the quiet room located only a few doors down from my homeroom class. The room was tiny, no larger than a walk-in closet, and unremarkable inside. White cinder blocks lined the walls throughout, the ceiling was unfinished, with one exceptionally long, bright fluorescent light hanging above. The first time I was sent to the quiet room, I was not alone. My long-time friend from elementary school and I had experienced a laughing fit which disrupted the learning of our classmates. We were sternly instructed to take our books to the little room, tucked away in the corner of the large classroom just a few doors down, and spent the remainder of the period in silence.

Being sent to the room was humiliating, but I was grateful to not be alone since I experienced a physical reaction to being placed in the small space. An immediate feeling of nervousness and nausea took over my entire body.

My homeroom teacher had been using the quiet room as a crutch to help manage unruly students whose behavior couldn't be controlled in the classroom, often sending children to a secluded time-out for the most minor of offenses. When the punishment of sitting alone in the hallway didn't work, there was always the quiet room. I would come to know the inside of that cold room very well, spending many lonely hours tucked away from the safety net of my peers and concealed from the watchful eye of the other educators in our school. Initially, my teacher would invite me back to the classroom within ten minutes, but after a while, that wasn't the case. Soon it wouldn't be uncommon for me to sit out for the entire period, and sometimes I would spend hours alone in that room.

During one of these trips, I noticed something unusual about the quiet room door that has never left me: the disturbing clicking sound the door made when it closed, reminiscent of the sound of a subway gate opening and closing with each passenger. There was a small window cut-out, oddly placed high up on the door, with a distinctive pattern made of tiny mesh triangles sandwiched between two glass panels. I can still remember counting those little triangles and standing on my tippy-toes to peek outside the window and catch a glimpse of the time on a large clock that hung on the wall of the outside classroom. Time went by so slowly in the quiet room, with little to do and nobody to socialize with. I passed the time by playing little games by myself, softly speaking aloud while counting to one hundred in groups of five: five, ten, fifteen, twenty . . .

I always felt tired while inside the quiet room but would quickly perk up when I heard the familiar sound of a jingling keyring and the patterned beat his feet made shuffling across the classroom floor, stopping just outside the quiet room door. It wasn't my homeroom teacher returning to dismiss me but a trusted confidant in the school who had decided now would be a suitable time to pay me another visit. I had a history of uncomfortable run-ins with this person, but I doubt my homeroom teacher could have imagined the role his decision to send me to the quiet room would play in my pain as a child. How this well-intentioned behavioral correction—sending me down the hall for a simple time-out—left me vulnerable to an enemy lurking in our school hallways. A person I confided in and shared all my childhood secrets with. A man who fooled me through his professional guise as the trusted confidant.

THE TRUSTED CONFIDANT

Chances are you've encountered someone just like him in your everyday interaction: a larger-than-life personality who makes you feel valued and special. That fun adult who lets you and your friends get away with things you know you shouldn't. An authoritative ally who takes the time to listen to your problems and intervene when you're faced with challenges too difficult to tackle alone.

But what they likely haven't yet taught you in the classroom is how to protect yourself from an unspoken danger.

The same person who possesses these wonderful, stand-out qualities *could also* be a dangerous child predator who uses their position of trust to gain intimate access to you. It is time to acknowledge an uncomfortable reality: the greatest risk to children comes from the people we trust and places we frequent. Unfortunately, this means that some of your own homes, schools, and sports clubs are unsafe environments that can house people detrimental to your well-being.

My generation was trained to be aware of "stranger danger," which is essentially the idea that you will remain safe as a child if you don't interact with people who are unknown to you. While avoiding strangers is a proven safety strategy, however, it simply deflects from the bigger threat facing our children. Most people that abuse children are not strangers waiting for a chance encounter in a dark alleyway at night. They are often well-liked members of our community, the people you already know and interact with every day.

- Parents
- Family members
- Friends
- Teachers
- Coaches
- Spiritual leaders

Abuse happens in many forms that cause physical or emotional harm to children and youth:

- Emotional abuse
- Exposure to violence
- Physical abuse
- Neglect
- Sexual abuse
- Cyber abuse

It is important for you to know that not every adult who pays attention to you is a predator or has bad intentions. In fact, most adults within your schools and activity centers are deeply caring people who have received special training to protect you from these situations. There have also been many positive advancements in the effort to reduce cases of childhood victimization, including the development of a mandatory sexual abuse prevention program required of all Certified Ontario Teachers that launched on January 1, 2022.

The goal of this chapter is not to scare you or make you distrust adults. I want you to be empowered within your daily environment and use discernment when faced with challenging situations or safety concerns.

You have the right to a safe environment free from abuse and violence.

You have the right to express yourself without the fear of judgment or bullying.

Adults should always respect your personal space and not engage with you in inappropriate ways.

You have the right to have your voice heard and concerns addressed in a timely manner.

Grooming Behaviour

At first, I liked the attention. He made a point to compliment my artwork and encouraged me to try out for the competitive gymnastics team. I relied on him for help navigating a difficult social environment with peers and to act as a go-between with my parents when I got in trouble. As an adult, I can now look back on my early interactions with this trusted confidant and recognize the grooming behavior and how it prepared me for what was to come.

- Early dismissal from class
- Physical roughhousing
- Unwanted touching
- Inappropriate comments about my body
- Crude jokes
- Talking about sex
- Providing gifts

Snapshot of a Youth in Crisis:

1) Sudden behavioral changes (changes in mood, communication, and functioning)

2) A dramatic physical transformation (eats less/more, weight loss/gain, neglects appearance, altered appearance, appears tired, unable to sleep)

3) Unhealthy coping mechanisms such as food, drugs, alcohol, or self-harm (increased risk-taking, experimenting, increased sexual behavior)

4) Avoidance behavior (fear of school, skipping school, running away from home)

5) Loss of concentration or engagement (quitting sports, changing friend groups, avoiding parents, decrease in engagement with teachers)

THE REALIZATION

I had forgotten all about that horrible quiet room and the bad things that took place in there when my memory was suddenly triggered at the most inopportune time. It was during a planned hospital stay to give birth to my first child that I made a horrifying connection. The door to the quiet room was just like the privacy door in my birthing suite: the kind of door specifically built to conceal the activity taking place inside so no one could see in during your most private and vulnerable moments. An overwhelming sense of fear came over me as I lay in the hospital bed, recovering from a difficult birth while staring off into the distance at the hospital door.

All I could think about was, "What if these rooms still exist?"

It was during that hospital stay that I realized it came down to the dangerous environment I had been placed in, and not just one bad apple at fault for my trauma as a child. My adult brain had always come to the rescue when exploring those terrible memories, as if to spare me the heartache of having to revisit the sadness of my youth and mourn the many losses from all those years ago.

But when I was in the seventh grade, I believed *I was the reason for all the heartache and blamed myself for the trauma I had to endure.*

It was a long night in the hospital. I didn't sleep a wink as I cuddled my precious baby until the sun came up, trying to come down from the feeling of euphoria that radiated throughout my body: that special feeling of becoming a first-time mom. I scanned every detail of my son's perfect body, creating a snapshot of each unique feature so I would never forget him.

Thoughts turned to memories of my own mother and the happy times we had once shared. Did she love me as much as I loved him? As much as your parents love you?

Something inside of me began to soften, and an unexpected trauma shift occurred. I saw myself for the first time as a twelve-year-old girl, through the lens of my own son's innocence. I started to reject the narrative assigned to me during the crisis I faced in the seventh grade; that I was simply just another bratty, out-of-control kid in desperate need of some tough love. The truth is, I was never a wild child. I was a traumatized child running wild and looking for a soft place to land.

RED FLAGS

Despite missing months of fundamental learning and falling behind academically, I was put through the system to the eighth grade and began the process of transforming into a tough new version of myself that was nothing like the little girl from the year before.

My morphed physical appearance and in-your-face behavior didn't improve my interactions with the trusted confidant, and the abuse continued into eighth grade. The situation had grown so dire that I would do anything to avoid being sent to school. I ran away frequently, missing 125 out of 150 days of class before I caught the attention of a senior school official who became responsible for my discipline and truancy file.

This was the lifeline I had been waiting for.

I took to him immediately and agreed to spend the remaining months of the school year working in the seventh grade classroom to catch up with my previously missed workload. It was like being held back a year since I was no longer with my original peer group each day for class. I started talking freely with him about many of my dysfunctional experiences at the school and felt reassured to finally have someone on my side.

What happened next was the worst betrayal I've experienced in my life.

I still can't bring myself to write about the last conversation I had in the main office or find the words to express how utterly heartbreaking it was for me as an adult to read the extensive case notes that documented my youth crisis. The conversation abruptly shifted as the focus became the need for me to remain positive and start fresh at a new school.

In March 1997, I was transferred away from the middle school with the cool blue roof, never having formally graduated from either grade seven or eight. The graduation yearbook remains a painful reminder of the emptiness I felt while walking out of those doors for the last time. An empty square with my name next to it. It was as if I had died, and nobody even noticed.

But I didn't die—I had survived the seventh grade and slowly began the process of rebuilding my life in a new community far away from my childhood pain.

I became laser-focused on building a brighter future which, I believed, was just around the corner. I got married, reunited with my favorite childhood sport as a gymnastics coach, and opened my first business—all before celebrating my *nineteenth birthday.*

The problem was, no matter where I relocated, who I surrounded myself with, or how many activities I tried to cram into the day, nothing ever seemed to work out. I couldn't erase from my memory the disturbing history from middle school. I began to question whether the life I was fighting so hard to establish was meant for someone else entirely.

Had I really chosen this path for myself, or was it simply a manifestation of unresolved trauma?

Why was it easier to avoid a family that loved me rather than share my pain?

Why did I choose to become a teenage bride in an unhappy relationship?

Why was I adverse to an academic path despite a natural aptitude for learning?

Why were memories of cherished childhood friends still so fresh in my mind even though I hadn't seen them in over twenty years?

Life throws unexpected curveballs, and sometimes you get hit by a low blow or two, or three! By the age of twenty-two, I was divorced and found myself in a deeply reflective state, navigating newly found adult independence. This time allowed me to process everything that I had endured. It was like a light switch went on as I reconnected with my twelve-year-old self and made her a promise. I knew that for me to move forward on the path I had always deserved, I would first need to revisit my past and set some things straight. I was introduced to a wonderful woman who specialized in childhood sexual abuse recovery and quickly realized that many of my ongoing struggles were linked to those traumatic years from middle school.

It was time to do something about it. I met with police to purge all the childhood secrets that had haunted me for so long, releasing myself from the weight of those burdens forever.

In 2019, I launched an investigation and legal action against the institution entrusted with my care. I found unexpected forgiveness through the legal process when the case was resolved in 2021 and have since shared my story with school board officials and child protection agencies to ensure that my experience could not be repeated in your modern learning environment.

With the support of my parents and brother, I went back to school and shifted gears professionally. I've been lucky to carve out some beautiful new memories with childhood friends I once thought were forever lost. I remarried, had two children, and settled into a quiet life on the outskirts of my hometown, forever cementing myself to the nickname by which I'm affectionately referred to in my community: *The Urban Runaway.*

Kids grow up. Power dynamics change. Disempowered youth become empowered adults. To anyone struggling to survive a rough adolescence, I see you, and I'm glad you're here! Don't ever stop believing that there is hope for a brighter future or let the bad things that happen to you alter the thousands of unique characteristics that make you incredibly special.

We all experience times in our life when we feel a bit lost. Just remember, you are never truly alone. Somewhere buried deep within each of you is a little white light just waiting to glow during your greatest time of need.

CHAPTER REFLECTION
FOR YOUTH:

1) Can you identify unsafe physical spaces within your daily environment that have the potential to become dangerous for your peer group?

2) Would you know how to tell if an adult in a position of authority is misusing their power or performing actions that put you at risk?

3) Could you identify a friend within your peer circle who is struggling and in need of help?

4) Have you ever witnessed behavior that made you feel uncomfortable but didn't say anything because you weren't sure who to tell?

REFLECTION QUESTIONS FOR ADULTS:

1) Have you ever believed an adult version of events over the recollection of a child?

2) Would you be able to recognize unusual behavior between an adult and child?

3) Do you believe you can take comprehensive steps today to further protect your children, starting with asking your child's school or activity program what effective abuse prevention policies they have in place?

4) Are you aware that everyone in Ontario is required by law to report suspected child abuse or neglect?

If you're in immediate danger, call 911.

If you have concerns about a child, call the Children's Aid Society.

To learn more about abuse prevention and support for survivors, contact Urban Runaway.

Chapter six

Lost & Found

"To truly nourish the soul, generously give compassion and mercy to all. Most importantly, to yourself."

Leah Marie Scott

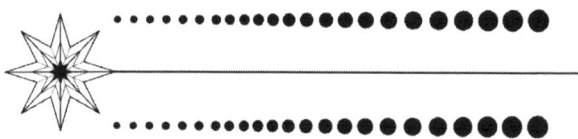

Fb: SMARTRecoveryFFCalgary
Fb: leahscott
Ig: lovebreathedesigns

Leah Marie Scott

Leah is a free-spirited lover of all things who thrives on mothering her three beautiful children and helping those in desperate need of clarity through the confusion and pain of struggling with addiction and loving someone with addiction. She currently resides in Calgary, Alberta, not far from where she grew up. After observing in her own life what a lack of love can do to a child, she is passionate about raising her children with an overabundance of unconditional love and acceptance so they can flourish and be shining lights for others without having to recover from their childhood.

Watching those around her battle addictions for most of her life, and struggling herself with the anxiety and depression that came with loving someone who struggled so deeply, Leah decided to seek an education in the field in order to be better equipped to make a real difference. Since she received her diploma (with honors) in 2017 for addictions and community service work, she has been working with SMART Recovery, a non-profit organization. where she teaches cognitive behavioral therapy and rational emotive behavioral therapy tools to those struggling with addiction and the ones who love them. Leah also teaches Smart Recovery tools for the Sobriety Home Foundation based out of Quebec and Nova Scotia.

> "The question is not why the addiction,
> but why the pain." -Gabor Mate

I grew up in what many considered the "ghetto" of my city. It was an intimidating place to those on the outside looking in, but like most things in life, it wasn't as scary as it appeared. At least not for me. Oddly enough, I felt quite safe in that world.

In hindsight, I can see how unsafe it really was. We had a high incidence of crime, and my high school had one of the worst graduation rates in the city. It was not uncommon to see homeless people talking to themselves on the corner or questionable-looking individuals hiding behind dumpsters. At a very young age, I remember hearing about my neighbor whose father shot and killed himself in the bathroom of my elementary school. Walking home from school, I would often hear my friend's father yelling and screaming, and I can remember walking into another friend's home that reeked of booze and where there were grown men passed out on the couch. She said she didn't even know who they were; apparently this was a regular occurrence in her home.

Many of my friends had physically abusive parents. Verbally and psychologically abusive as well, but those scars are much less obvious. I had friends who were gang members. I lost some friends to drive-by shootings and violence that would break out at parties. One day as I was sitting in my grade ten English class, I heard some chaotic muffles coming from the hallway. After seeing my teacher in a panic, I walked out to see a friend of mine drenched in blood. His face was hardly recognizable. I never saw him again after that.

Most of my guy friends eventually became gang members or were affiliated with gangs. By the time we reached high school, many of my friends were consuming alcohol as a regular passtime. Drugs were a normal part of our existence. I would drink at parties, but that was the extent for me. Many of the boys however, were snorting cocaine or smoking crack.

I suppose, considering all the misery, death, and violence I grew up witnessing, my childhood community *is* what most would consider a ghetto. Perhaps the reason I was able to stay detached from all the darkness that surrounded me was because my home was a safe, loving space, which meant my base foundation was stable. Venturing out into such a dark world wasn't as ground-shaking for me. I'm sure I also normalized it. We humans adapt well to our environments. Being so little, I had no basis for comparison. All the dysfunction was quite normal in my eyes. I'm sure it also helped that there were little gems of loving folk hidden in the dark. Old, gentle, kind couples or single ladies whose houses felt like home. So many moments of laughter and joy with my family members and friends. Kind, encouraging teachers. And not all my friends had troubled homes. Some had very loving homes much like mine, and I would naturally gravitate more toward them.

My mother raised me and my three siblings by herself. She moved from a small town in Saskatchewan to attend college, where she met my father. After many years of trying to make it work with him, his battle with alcohol addiction was too much, and my mother left him when I was just a baby. Despite the fact that we were financially poor, my childhood was rich with love. My home was warm and welcoming. My mom was a stable mother figure. I knew, without a doubt, that I was loved and accepted just as I was. And my life thus far, with my personal experiences as well as my education and continued work in the addictions field, has taught me what a gift that really is. Isn't that what we all want—need, in fact? To feel seen and heard and accepted? Unconditionally loved? Especially by the ones who brought us into this world. I witnessed many times, through observing friends around me, just how much tragedy can come from a lack of unconditional love in a child's home.

My father's childhood was lacking in love, to say the least. But even though he wasn't in the picture much of the time because of his struggles with addiction, his rare words of wisdom and random thoughtful birthday cards and gifts assured me that he was there, if I ever really needed him. He broke the vicious cycle of abuse he experienced in his childhood.

Perhaps that was easier for him to accomplish because my mother left him when my siblings and I were so little. He was left to deal with his darkness alone; we weren't around for him to abuse on his worst days, of which I imagine he had many. I believe it was a wise choice on my mother's part, and I am happy to report that my father has been sober for twenty years. My hope for anyone struggling with addiction remains strong because of this.

My mother's home was like a diamond in the rough. It wasn't just a safe space for those of us dwelling there; her non-judgmental energy was inviting for our friends and all the kids in the neighborhood. None of us ran away from my mother's home (I mean, we threatened to at times, but that was mostly due to sibling rivalry than anything my mother was doing). No, our home was the place our friends ran away *to*. And my mother didn't seem to mind much. She didn't ask many questions. Perhaps because she grew up in small-town Saskatchewan, her mental range for potential danger wasn't accurately reflective of the city's "ghetto" life. Dangers lurked, no doubt, but she didn't seem too scared for us. Her mind just didn't think that way.

Because of this, we were allowed to journey our neighborhood to our hearts' content. Explore. Be individuals. Have the friends we wanted. I think this was why none of us rebelled against her like so many kids do, like so many of my friends did. Throughout my childhood, I observed that the stricter and more overbearing the parents, the more rebellious the child. In other words, the more fearful the parent, the more the child yearned to be free.

I also spent a great deal of my childhood in my best friend's home. We met the first day of first grade and were inseparable. My mother was too busy working and trying to survive and provide for her four children to be able to treat us to many forms of entertainment and wholesome family outings. Many of these things I was gifted by Jessie and her family: going to the movies, the Boys and Girls Club, the leisure center, camping, jet skiing at her aunt's lake house. They fed me dinner many nights as well. They say it takes a village to raise a child. I had a pretty good village. I'm still somewhat processing and grieving and therefore very sad to report that Jessie died of a drug overdose on February

9, 2022, three days before my thirty-eighth birthday. She leaves behind her five beautiful sons.

While my home life was good, though, I was not without my own personal adversities. I dealt with a few bullies, and I just want to say to that right now: stand up to them. Look them in the eye. Bullies prey on the weak. They will back down if you find the courage to stand up.

I was heavy for most of my youth, which contributed greatly to my self-esteem issues. I experienced a lot of rejection from boys. I was introverted and shy, which led to nervous breakdowns in certain situations. I was deemed too quiet and felt quite judged for it. I had acne and, like most teenagers, struggled with teen angst and depression. We were financially poor, so the pressure of feeling "less-than" when around my friends who had money contributed to feeling somewhat devalued.

After losing weight and becoming more confident as a young lady, I spent most of my twenties dating "lost boys." They say you are drawn to lovers who are most like your parent of the opposite sex (or the sex you are attracted to). So considering my father's personal struggles with alcohol, it is really no surprise that the man I fell madly in love with and created two gorgeous humans with indeed had his own dark cloud of addiction hovering. I met him when I was twenty-six. My previous three relationships entailed mass confusion and had ended in heartbreak, which fostered a deep desperation for love and fear of rejection. It blinded me. The flags were indeed there, but my fear of abandonment, of rejection, of not being enough encouraged me to turn my cheek to the very obvious signs. Our story is for another book; all you need to know is that, in the words of Elizabeth Gilbert in *Eat, Pray, Love*, "I dove into his arms exactly the same way a cartoon circus performer dives off a high platform and into a small cup of water, vanishing completely."

Because of the heartbreak I had already experienced, my self-esteem was rather low, and my sense of self-worth was tied solely to him—and he was a mess of a human being. So you can guess what that meant for me. I fell into a dark place of depression and anxiety. A place I didn't recognize. A place I had never been before in my life. I lost all sense of joy. I lost Leah. At one point, I actually believed I was losing my mind. I had this overwhelming desperation to run as fast as I could, as far as I could, but the problem was I couldn't run away from my mind.

Turns out, the fear of insanity was "just" severe mental exhaustion from trying to pour from an empty cup for too long. And I was so occupied with trying to fill his. Why? Because addiction is on the corner of pity-party central. The more you use to cope with the pain, the worse you feel. I became consumed with making sure he was okay so that I could feel okay, and he was rarely okay. You might be thinking he must have been a monster for me to lose myself to such an extent, and in all honesty he appeared quite monstrous to me at times, but no. He was a man with a big heart. The monster was his addiction.

This was the first time I prayed to God. The one time I had attempted prayer in my teenage years, I was not in a place of desperation, and I found myself intimidated by it, afraid I wouldn't pray the right way. So I gave up. This time, though, standing in the shower feeling more lost and filled with fear than ever before, I begged God to tell me why I was here. Why I was feeling this way. I didn't give a fuck how I spoke to Him or Her or It or this intelligent energetic force. I just needed to know what the fuck this all was for.

For the first time in my life, I was desperate to understand the meaning of my existence and I demanded answers. As far as I knew at the time, I didn't choose to be here. Someone or something put me here, and I deserved to know why. Slowly, but surely answers appeared. Clarity came to me in comments made by friends and family. A book my mother brought over, and other books I came across. Encounters with wiser beings than myself. Music and lyrics. I came across spiritual mentors I had never heard of before. Slowly I started to see how I had gotten so lost and eventually realized that I had more to do with it than I thought—and that therefore, I had much more power to change it than I had thought. Ultimately, my darkness led me to find God, to find the spiritual dimension within myself. The darkness led me to the light. It brought me to my faith.

Eventually my relationship ended. I couldn't take watching the man I loved self-destruct. No matter how hard I tried to "save" him from himself, he wasn't ready or willing. Our daughters deserved better. I deserved better. Around the same time we split, I found out my best friend Jessie had been struggling with an addiction to fentanyl. As soon as I found out, I forced her into a detox center. Hard lesson learned: don't force your beliefs on someone when they are not ready. She didn't speak to me for about two years. We started talking again when she sought recovery herself. When she was ready.

I had three long, lovely visits with her through the time she was in recovery, ones I will cherish for the rest of my life. All I could see at that time was struggling souls around me, like I had always seen in childhood, only now it seemed so much worse. I decided to seek out an education to further my knowledge so I could contribute productively to finding solutions. If the house you're in is burning to the ground, you get up and get water. You get as much water as you can carry.

I received my diploma in addictions and community service work, graduating with honors. The best thing to come out of my college experience was learning about a non-profit organization by the name of SMART Recovery. I did my practicum through Smart Recovery Calgary and I continue to volunteer with them to this day. The humility, compassion, and love I felt in that room every night during those SMART Recovery meetings was an experience I will never forget. It was the humility that can only come from falling flat on your face and finding the courage to get back up. We all fall. We will all get lost at some point in this complicated life, many times in fact, but we can also rise. We will find ourselves again, and oh my, the rise can be magnificent. And no matter how far you fall, you can always find your way out if it's what you truly want. Rock bottom can be a gift.

These days, I run Smart family and friends support meetings because struggling with an addiction is a hellish experience but loving someone who struggles with addiction is a kind of hell on its own, and I relate more to the latter.

At SMART, we teach cognitive behavioral therapy and rational emotive behavioral therapy. I find these therapies to be the most beneficial to our complex human minds. They provide truly self-empowering knowledge! I am going to share my favorite tool with you, but know that it is just a peek. If you struggle with addiction or love someone who does, don't let fear hold you back from seeking help. I have found that doing the thing you are most afraid to do is where the real magic happens. We all have God-like qualities within us. We are all His children, after all. Find the courage within you, and you will be rewarded beyond what you can imagine. Following this chapter is the ABC tool. It is my favorite because it gives a simple answer to a very complex issue. It can help us regain control over our emotional upsets and shows us that we have control over how we feel. Our perception is everything. The way we think affects how we feel, which affects how we behave. The more aware we become of our thinking patterns, the more we are in control of how we feel rather than allowing external stimuli to determine that for us.

"I was lost but now am found/Was blind but now I see."

-Amazing Grace

THIS IS WHAT I'VE LEARNED:

Do not be afraid of the darkness within you. It is there for a very good reason. Mental exhaustion from chronic stress will bring on very dark thoughts, but they are just as natural as the lighter, happier thoughts. You are not going crazy, and there is nothing wrong with you. Rest your weary mind. Seek guidance, even (especially) from above. You are not alone.

It is of vital importance to feel like we have purpose and meaning in our lives. Find what you love and do it. At SMART, we teach an acronym VACI, which stands for Vitally Absorbing Creative Interests. Do the things that anchor you into the moment. Meditation is where it's at, but if you're not open to that, doing the things you truly enjoy will surely suffice. Don't get caught up in doing just what you have to do. Burnout is real, so fill your cup every day. Self-care is self-love. I learned how to fill my own cup. How absolutely vital it is to my flourishment in life. The pain I went through showed me how strong I really was and what I wasn't paying attention to: myself and what I needed.

We have much more control over our emotions than most of us are aware of. We can learn how to control our emotional upsets and deal with life's challenges in a much calmer and more confident manner. It helps to think back to a time you didn't think you would get through— remember that you did in fact get through it. You may not recall exactly how you did it, but like a kind of magic, answers and solutions came, and you found your way through the dark.

We are all humans, brothers and sisters, and when we can recognize ourselves in another, it bridges the gap and helps us to trust in others enough to be more open and receptive instead of fearful. Fear can paralyze us; it can and will hold us back from being our best selves and from doing the things that we know we are capable of doing.

Our creator is listening. Seek and you shall find.

All the things I perceived as "bad" that happened in my life were gifts. They woke me up to what I wasn't aware of. I am who I am, and I love who I am, because I fell flat on my face and I found the courage to get back up. We get to choose how we handle life's challenges. We can allow them to make us stronger or pummel us to the ground.

Addiction is people's way of escaping from the feelings and thoughts they don't want to experience. We may feel like we can't bear those thoughts and feelings, but we can, if only we could sit with them long enough to understand why they are there. No feeling or thought is final. They always pass. One of the most important things I have learned is how to sit with my discomfort instead of attempting to run away. What we perceive as our "bad" thoughts and feelings won't just fade away. They are there to offer us a deeper understanding of ourselves, if we could just listen, and they need to be felt and processed. Otherwise they stew and come out in uglier ways. Your feelings, no matter how terrifying, will not annihilate you.

I am not completely free from anxiety, nor will I ever be. This world is mysterious. Uncertain. But my strong faith gives me the courage and clarity I need to deal with my moments of fear. Your life has meaning. You are a child of God. Express yourself in whichever way feels good to you, and trust the answers will come.

The How To; (Removable attachment)

The ABC Model

A = Activating event

B = Our Beliefs/perceptions about the event

C = Consequences of our feelings or behaviors

It is easy to be unaware of our B (Beliefs/perceptions) and think that an A (Activating event) simply leads automatically to the C (Consequences). However, there is always a thought or a B (Belief) that precedes a response. It is the thought or belief that leads to the C (Consequences), not the A (Activating event) itself.

Example:

Consider how Person 1 and Person 2 experience different reactions and consequences as a result of the same activating event:

Person 1:

A = Gets stuck in a traffic jam on the way out to dinner.

B = "This is terrible! I can't stand this. I will be late, and that is just unforgivable."

C = Becomes stressed. Arrives tense and in a bad mood and ends up complaining about the traffic, which turns into an argument.

Person 2:

A = Gets stuck in a traffic jam on the way out to dinner.

B = "The traffic is out of my control. There is no point getting upset. I will listen to some relaxing music and calmly apologize for the inconvenience as soon as I arrive."

C = Arrives in a relaxed state, smiling. Apologizes and indulges in a nice conversation.

Being aware of your thoughts, beliefs, and perceptions can help you to challenge them, thereby allowing you to reduce your psychological distress and change your habitual ways of responding to difficult situations.

CHAPTER SEVEN

ROBOTS DON'T EAT COOKIES

*"The Pursuit of Perfection Is Just
a Distraction"*

Mary FR Smith

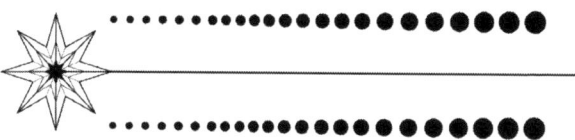

www.marysmithparentcoach.com
Fb (personal): mfrsmith
Fb (business): marysmithparentcoach
Fb (private group): marysmithparentgroup
Ig: marysmithparentcoach
LI: mary-smith4
Youtube: marysmithparentcoach
Goodreads: goodreads.com/author/show/22956974.
Mary_FR_Smith

Mary FR Smith

Mary FR Smith is a compassionate, kind, say-it-as-it-is person who loves humor and people. Her complicated experience as a parent to four girls just five years apart prompted her to shift her profession to one dedicated to empowering and motivating parents to be confident in their role, enjoy parenting, and build resilient families.

Mary is an accomplished businesswoman, a Master Certified Life Coach, a Certified Positive Discipline Expert, and a multi-published parenting author. She is frequently on tour as a public speaker for schools, corporations, and parent groups.

Despite a chaotic upbringing and, later, bouts of parental overwhelm, shame, and perfectionism, Mary achieved positive change. She developed a passion for neuroscience, mindfulness, and child development which led to her thesis that understanding emotions and the processes of a child's brain that drive behavior is fundamental to success as a parent. She has since set out to simplify this for parents.

Mary's passion lies in reversing the rising tide of teen and young adult anxiety and depression, which she believes, for parents and children, starts with a moment of connection.

I n September of my senior year in high school, I was hanging around outside the locker rooms before heading out to field hockey practice. My friend Greg, also a senior and fellow athlete, appeared and apparently felt compelled to confess, "I was going to vote for you for homecoming queen, but, you know, you win everything. I thought I should give someone else a chance."

He didn't intend to be mean. I didn't actually take it as mean. Maybe it was true.

The apple never falls far from the tree. Forty years later, I asked my third daughter why she wanted to quit ballet to swim. With the matter-of-factness of a six-year-old, she replied, "Because you can't win at ballet."

Perfectionism

And it's not just my daughters. More and more young people are internalizing the contemporary myth that things, including themselves, should be perfect.[1]

- Win anything and everything.
- Look perfect on social media.
- Don't let emotions get the better of you.
- Get A's. Be popular. Be attractive. Be kind.
- Always pursue success . . . regardless of cost.

What's not to like? People with high levels of perfectionism tend to be ambitious, hard-working, and diligent[2], right? Well, sort of. Stretching one's skills and pursuing excellence are not

---

1   T. Curran and A.P. Hill, "Perfectionism Is Increasing and That's No Good News," Harvard Business Review, January 26, 2018, https://hbr.org/2018/01/perfectionism-is-increasing-and-thats-not-good-news.
2   Ibid.

inherently bad. But somewhere along the line, striving for perfection goes sideways; being flawless becomes our hustle to feeling worthy of love and belonging. But we aren't robots operating under a set of conditions and outcomes. We are human beings. We experience, act, and react through our visceral, sometimes unpredictable, emotions, not through algorithm-driven actions.

YOUNG CHILDHOOD

I grew up the fifth of six children. Apparently I didn't require a lot of attention. My mother left me in the crib for hours because I never complained. Elementary school teachers seated me among rambunctious boys because I was a peacemaker. My father rubbed his chin and looked very concerned if I had one less-than-stellar mark on my kindergarten report card. I was affable, bright, cute, and easy.

My father was a brilliant trial lawyer. My mother was beautiful, hard-working, and kind. We lived in an idyllic house on the hill, rode our own horses, and played tennis at the club.

My father was also an alcoholic, paranoid, abusive, and bipolar. My mother was tolerant, overwhelmed, and scared. Our homelife was one where chaos was the norm, and there were many times when my siblings and I simply couldn't count on our parents.

Skipping my way through the first twelve years of life, I conveniently shunned the dysfunction.

Every afternoon, after the school bus pulled away, my siblings and I would race up the long driveway and into the house, eager for a snack. One day we discovered my dad sitting at the kitchen table, disheveled and smelling of whiskey, sawing the shotguns (we had them for protecting livestock) in half. He explained that he was worried he might shoot all of us.

I went and got a cookie.

On a clear fall day, I wrote, "Dear Diary, Today Daddy didn't go to work. He sat in the study all day with the shades down, even though the leaves are so pretty. I saw a big black-and-blue bump over his eye. I heard Mom smashing bottles. I think that means he's drinking again so Tommy and I stayed in the attic and played Monopoly. Love, Mary."

I ate another cookie.

When I was eleven, my father took his life. I found out when my neighbor explained why so many people were delivering flowers and food.

There were lots of yummy sweets.

TRAUMA

Most people think of trauma as caused only by big events, such as rape, war, or the death of a loved one. But traumas are not measured by what happens on the outside. Trauma simply means that we were not able to handle the processing of emotions around an event at the time, particularly during periods of brain development like early childhood and adolescence. Emotions are either processed by feeling or experiencing them to release them, or they are suppressed and they simmer. It's that festering that's the precursor to stress, anxiety, and/or depression.

The thing is, we all have a unique coping capacity to handle stress, based on our temperament, environment, and genetics. Understanding trauma's impact is more about how it affects you and less about the event itself.[3]

In my case, being capable, brave, and resilient were in my favor, but the sorrow and shame that accompanied my fathers' death weren't welcome. So I learned to harness my emotions or, possibly, not allow myself to have them at all. I distracted myself by striving to be the perfect child, to soothe and not dwell on any unpleasant feelings.

And when I couldn't, there were always cookies.

---

3   Substance Abuse and Mental Health Services Administration (SAMHSA) 2014, Trauma-Informed Care in Behavioral Health Services. Treatment Improvement Protocol (TIP) Series 57. HHS Publication No. (SMA) 13-4801. Rockville, MD: Substance Abuse and Mental Health Services Administration.

The problem is that perfectionism masquerades as a coping mechanism. In "therapy-speak," a coping mechanism is something that we do to deal with negative emotions in a healthy way. Journaling or deep breathing can help to manage stress. To cope.

For me, perfectionism was more like what those same therapists would call a compensatory strategy. We opt to do something with conviction to avoid something else. I could excel so I didn't have to feel. I *could* be a robot. On the surface, these strategies can equip us to "keep going," but they don't resolve the root problems. Sadly, they just perpetuate the pain and confusion, impeding one's ability to lead an authentic life.

MIDDLE SCHOOL

I kept skipping along. I became a plucky little middle-schooler with a ponytail, chest out, ready to conquer anything in my way. I achieved a string of A's, excelled at sports, and had plenty of friends.

And since my father had just taken his own life, maybe, just maybe, I was a little bit angry.

My friends and I were evolving twelve-year-old girls and, despite our upbeat exteriors, we could be rebellious and mean. One Saturday in eighth grade, while rehearsing for the school play, a few of us found ourselves outside the gym teacher's office. In one of those, *I'm not sure what I was thinking,* moments, we scratched crude language into the door.

I was hurting and, like so many kids, I didn't have the words, much less the awareness, to articulate what needs aren't being met. (Imagine: "*Excuse me, Mom. I'm confused and hurt, even though it looks lik*e *I have everything under control; could someone make some time for me?*") Emotional needs aren't as obvious as being hungry or thirsty. So, without the words, behavior is very often children's way of communicating in the only way they know how. But adults aren't always great at understanding that.

The following Monday, I was the first student called to the principal's office. A dark cloud of disappointment and dread enveloped me, and I denied everything, vehemently. I was a good kid; this was impossible. Looking a beloved English teacher directly in the eye, I pleaded with her to believe that I hadn't slipped up and that I was a good, worthy girl.

Ultimately, the names came out. I wasn't allowed to play field hockey or be on the student council. They told my mother. She never spoke to me about it; she was petrified of upsetting what appeared to be an otherwise perfect apple cart.

High school was on the horizon, and I was never going to put myself in that position again.

EMOTIONS AND COPING

Parents who under-notice, under-value, or under-respond to their child's emotions inadvertently convey a powerful, subliminal message to the child: Your feelings don't matter; you (and I) don't need to pay attention to them.

But emotions direct us; they are there to guide, inform, connect, and enrich us. This is where we discover our authenticity: "gut" emotions are the gateway to *who* matters to you, *what* matters to you, and *why*.[4]

I'd come to associate winning with worthiness, and every moment of satisfaction served to fuel my belief that the outcome is paramount. The shame and pain of my little twelve-year-old's big mistake served to crystallize the all-or-nothing association between being perfect and being happy. Anything else was disappointment, pain, and shame.

Doing well is a good thing. Achieving is admirable when it manifests as working toward goals that stretch us. Taking on challenges, enjoying the process, having a sense of preparedness, getting comfortable with uncertainty, and celebrating the little successes are all part of growth while attaining an objective.

That is not to be confused with the pursuit of perfection, which is just a distraction. While I am striving to be the best,

4   J. Webb, "Seven Signs You Grew Up with Childhood Emotional Neglect," PsychCentral, July 23, 2017, https://psychcentral.com/blog/childhood-neglect/2017/07/7-signs-you-grew-up-with-childhood-emotional-neglect#7-Signs-You-Grew-Up-With-Childhood-Emotional-Neglect.

I can ignore those uncomfortable emotions that I either don't want to or can't acknowledge: the emptiness, the fear of being dependent, the loneliness, the lack of self-compassion, the constant guilt and shame. I'm going to do everything right and win everything—then I'll be worthy of acceptance and belonging.

FRESHMAN YEAR

I practiced field hockey all summer long and made the varsity team. It was a start. I continued to be an honors student, captained multiple varsity sports teams, set a running record, played saxophone in the marching band, babysat to earn my own money, and was kind and well-liked. The robotic algorithm required success. I was on course.

At home, when one of my brothers, feeling jealousy, beat me up, I baked cookies.

I ran for class president in my freshman year. I lost. I ran against the same girl sophomore and junior years, losing both times, validating that the three-time winner, my friend, was our class's respected and rightful leader.

Then it was senior year. *"When I am perfect, I will feel safe and secure"* had become an internalized belief, my unconscious story. If I could be flawless, I would be worthy, complete, loved. To be flawless, I *needed to win everything and be number one.*

LIFETRAPS

Children have hard-wired emotional needs (safety, autonomy, connection to others, self-esteem, self-expression, and realistic limits) that have to be met in order to thrive and become well-adjusted adults. Our needs not being met in just the Goldilocks-right amount provides the fodder for our stories. That story, coined a "lifetrap" by Jeffrey Young, is, simply put, a self-defeating pattern of thoughts, emotions, and behaviors that keep us stuck. "They began with something that was "done" to us by our families or other children.

We were neglected, abandoned, criticized, overprotected, abused, excluded, or deprived—we were damaged in some way."[5]

Hold on: my parents loved me. Your parents love you, fiercely. But, despite good intentions, perfection in parenting is also impossible because—wait for it— parents have *their* own stories. Lifetraps are, unfortunately, impossible to avoid. Blame doesn't heal. Blame just deepens the shame and perpetuates the trauma.

Eventually the lifetrap becomes part of us. "Long after we leave the home we grew up in, we continue to create situations in which we are mistreated, ignored, put down, or controlled and in which we fail to reach our most desired goals."[6] That doesn't mean we are all doomed. Generally speaking, the degree to which the child is either denied or given in excess any of these core needs is the degree to which he or she will struggle with a particular lifetrap.

But how lifetraps manifest in our life can be complex, in much the same way as trauma is more about the individual than the event. Two children can experience the same event, but the lifetrap and the degree of its impact is determined by how each child interprets what was "done" to him or her.

At their worst, lifetraps are formidable and enduring obstacles to authenticity. For example, burdening oneself with the pursuit of perfection is, cruelly, a double delusion: the end is elusive but even if one were to arrive, you haven't escaped from the clenches of the trap.

SENIOR YEAR

I didn't thoughtfully consider whether I wanted to be president or whether it was right for me at that moment. My thinking was binary; not running wasn't an option. A couple of friends urged me on, and I clung to their encouragement as justification for my actions despite a nagging feeling that I repressed with other emotional variables I'd habitually ignored.

---

5   Jeffrey Young and Janet Kiosko, 1994, Reinventing Your Life (New York, NY: Plume).

6   Ibid

I ran. By a slim margin, this time I won.

So why didn't it feel better? Don't get me wrong; *winning* felt great. But was this the "real me?" In my robotic quest for this success, had I compromised my core values, such as courage, humility, friendship, teamwork, and respect?

I distinctly remember the quintessential Friday evenings in September, working on the Homecoming float. An exhilarating aura of we-are-now-seniors and let's-make-this-amazing filled the big old barn on the outskirts of town. I led. I smiled. I joked. But the camaraderie with this entire group of really important classmates was not the same. If I had been voted most popular and the president of the class, why did I feel so lonely?

AUTHENTICITY

Authenticity relates to the congruence and consistency between our "real self," which is our actual behavior, and our "ideal self," which is who we would like to be. And our values are the attributes of the person we want to be. But values can be tricky. It's easy to be lured in by defining values as "what we care about," but simply ascribing importance to something in our lives, such as money, doesn't imply it's a value.

Here's a simple test: if someone can take it away from you, it's not a value.

We risk inauthenticity when we lose ourselves by outsourcing our behavior to an algorithm and then abdicating responsibility for the repercussions and their impact on our lives. Back to the money example. Money is something you care about, but whether you steal it or acquire it through honest work is based on your values. Get it? It takes conscious effort to identify and then override lifetraps, choosing values over following a scripted path, over fitting in[7].

---

7   S. Salicru, "Seven Practices to Become More Authentic," PsychCentral, October 19, 2021, https://www.psychologytoday.com/us/blog/psychology-insights-new-world/202110/7-practices-become-more-authentic.

At our thirty-year reunion, after welcoming everyone and thanking them for coming, I passed the microphone to my friend, the true leader of our class.

Evolving to an increasingly authentic life is like any learning process: it starts with reflection. Pause and become self-aware of who you are and then make the choice to continually challenge yourself. You can compassionately counter your flawed beliefs until those patterns loosen their grip on you.[8] Identify and celebrate each moment, however modest, that represents progress in your quest to decouple yourself from the crutches of robotic coping.

And if a cookie will fuel your journey to authenticity, go for it.

---

8   Adapted from J. Young, Reinventing Your Life, The Bestselling Breakthrough Program to End Negative Behaviour and Feel Great (New York: Plume, 1994), p.3.

HOW TO MOVE TOWARD AUTHENTICITY:

Identify your lifetrap. For an in-depth questionnaire and a non-technical, easy-to-understand explanation, I recommend reading Jeffrey E. Young's, *Reinventing Your Life, the Bestselling Breakthrough Program to End Negative Behaviour and Feel Great.*

Review the following list of some commonly held values:

- Authenticity
- Community
- Compassion
- Complexity
- Courage
- Creativity
- Faith
- Flexibility
- Generosity
- Gratitude
- Honesty
- Humility
- Humor
- Integrity
- Kindness
- Love
- Loyalty
- Open-Mindedness
- Optimism
- Perseverance
- Realism
- Simplicity
- Spontaneity
- Tenacity
- Thoughtfulness
- Tolerance
- Wisdom

Which do you think are most important? Select at least ten.

Highlight those that reflect who you are (your "real self") and circle those that you want to become (your "ideal self"). How aligned are they?

Reflect on how your "ideal self" values show up in your life currently and how you could incorporate them even further. For example, if one of your values is perseverance, you might ask yourself how you are embodying that attribute. Maybe you could add a stepping stone to your weekly goals. What more could you do to live by this value?

CHAPTER EIGHT

RUNNING AWAY

"If you become willing to entertain the thought that it could get better, then you're halfway there. It's only as hard as you make it."

Karla Torres

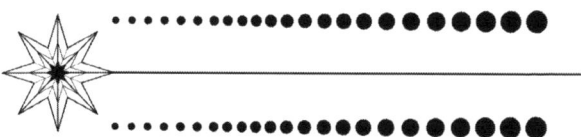

www.theawakenedmamas.com

Fb: Karlatorres.co
Ig: the_awakenedmama
Tiktok: theawakenedmama

Karla Torres

Karla had spent her life feeling unfulfilled, ashamed, and totally confused about where she was going. She was seeking answers to the emotional blocks and ways of thinking that caused her to put limitations on herself out of fear of failure, lack of awareness, and feeling lost in life. After being introduced to Neuro-Linguistic Programming (NLP), a life-changing experience, she soon realized her pain was what aligned her with her purpose. She learned she could make a true difference helping others find the answer to those same questions and doubts. As a Master NLP Practitioner and coach, Karla focuses on working with moms who are feeling lost or disconnected and experiencing rage in their motherhood experience. Karla uses NLP tools to see through the emotional cover of an issue right to its core. She helps her clients move forward with their lives by helping them recognize their worth and value and identify the beliefs that are holding them back, along with what they truly want and how to get it so they can reach their full potential. With the support of coaching and empowering tools and strategies, Karla's clients are able to get back their power and move toward the exciting future they desire and deserve.

RUNNING AWAY FROM YOUR PROBLEMS WON'T MAKE THEM GO AWAY.

Growing up in a toxic, unstable, unsafe home meant I learned to live with my circumstances to survive. Over time, that turned into PTSD. But I was so afraid to get lost in depression and end up in a hospital that I just decided to pretend not to know how bad things were and to avoid conflict, confrontation, and any other hard things.

If anything occurred to jeopardize my sanity or peace, I would shut down and internalize it deep in my core, until little by little, it would leak back to the surface in vulnerable situations.

In my relationships, I needed to be in control by having the last say on things. I couldn't handle being rejected, abandoned, or hurt yet again, so when things got tough, I would pull the plug. Almost like a pause on the inevitable. If I walked away before the end, then I never truly failed. It was my coping mechanism.

Unfortunately, with time, that belief turned into a pattern. How I managed my relationship with friends, family, and partners became how I handled everything, including school grades and jobs. I would drop out or quit to avoid stress, negative thoughts, and uncomfortable feelings. I learn to numb myself through distance, keeping myself busy and eventually becoming a workaholic. It was like escaping my reality. Almost a relief.

While this behavior served its purpose in keeping me sane, at ease, and in control of my life. It didn't address the root issue of it all. What I was doing was escaping, internally on a subconscious level.

SUBCONSCIOUS—SAY WHAT?

Yup, I know. I had no idea that my subconscious even played a role in my behavior. Turns out, though, our subconscious mind influences our all behaviors, actions, and reality.

The unconscious mind is a reservoir of feelings, thoughts, urges, and memories that are outside of our conscious awareness. The unconscious contains contents that are traumatic or unpleasant experiences and will do its best to repress those memories or feelings to avoid suffering or pain. Unfortunately, this becomes a pattern of behaviors that loops over and over until our unconscious mind can no longer hold space; then the body starts to leak or manifest these pain points in different ways as it looks for resolution.

My avoidance behavior started to manifest in my conscious life, but I had no awareness of what was happening. I just pretended like it wasn't happening and told myself to be strong and keep doing what I knew best.

I thought I had it all figured out!

In reality, though, I felt very alone in my thoughts, my connections, and my world. I felt isolated and not important to the people I love. I felt like I wasn't lovable and worthy of a better life. I felt like I was just cursed to live this life til the end of my time.

I had gotten so used to avoiding big feelings, uncomfortable conversations, and negative situations that I also missed out on good connections, memorable moments, and happy emotions. I subscribed to the belief that it wasn't safe to be vulnerable or to let people in for fear of rejection and abandonment. I would fall in love with the idea of being best friends or in a relationship forever—then I would hit a roadblock, and all the inner critic would say was, "Run before they get you or before you get hurt!" So I would pull back and find flaws or red flags to prove that I was right and that my heart could not be trusted in the hands of another.

Looking back, I can see how I contributed to my relationship failures. I either attracted the right people and pulled away or attracted the wrong people because I was always trying to prove that no one could pull the wool over my eyes and that having the upper hand meant I was safe. Boy, was I mistaken.

I didn't know this in my twenties, but it was almost as if I was experiencing a midlife crisis. I couldn't understand why I felt so disconnected and out of control. I had no idea where my life was headed or with whom, and nothing seemed to feel content or safe. I couldn't feel happy. No amount of money, job, or new relationship could take away the sorrow I felt in my soul.

I wish I knew in that moment that life could be different, that it didn't have to be this way. That my behaviors could be reprogrammed to serve me rather than limit me. Unfortunately, at that time, I did not have the know-how or tools to move past this point.

Being unaware of how I was contributing to my own pain led me down a path of emptiness.

I blamed everyone (and myself) for where my life was at that moment.

- I felt unsupported.
- I felt unloved.
- I felt ashamed
- I felt unworthy of a better life.
- I felt unsafe to be at peace or vulnerable and to receive love or give love.
- I suppressed my anger, fears, anxiety, and guilt.

I thought by controlling my emotions, I would be in control. It took me a while to figure out that that was a false sense of control. I was trying to forget that wounded little girl so bad I blocked her out.

I talked myself through the addiction of avoidance. "Just until I figure this out or until I land a good paying job." Then I would deal with my mental health. Every day was a challenge to try to keep it all together. I was exhausted and found myself numbing the pain through partying, overindulging, or binge-watching Netflix.

But that nagging feeling kept showing up: that feeling of being in a glass house, where one little pebble would shatter everything. Everything I didn't want was starting to surface.

I started having panic attacks, dizzy spells, and body dis-ease. My body started to manifest physical problems like chronic lower back pain. I had back spasms that would put me out of work and in bed for days. Even when I was in pain, though, I would try to work through it—until I learned my lesson and manifested a herniated bulging disk that took me six months to recover from.

Everything in my life stopped, and no amount of medication was going to fix it. I was desperate. I couldn't run away anymore. It was time to face my demons so that I could be free from my past, both the emotional baggage my mind was carrying and physical pain that came along with it.

I had no choice but to ask for help. Nothing I was doing was working anymore, and now I could end up losing my ability to walk.

I reached out to doctors, energy healers, everyone, and eventually was introduced to a group of humans who were healing from their traumas and using their pain as wisdom. I met a fascinating human being called Ernie who saw right through my pain and allowed me the opportunity to be a student, to learn how pain and trauma can be resolved through the unconscious mind rather than conscious mind. I learned that the mind that created the problem cannot create the solution.

It was no wonder I couldn't break my patterns on my own. I needed someone who could guide me and hold space for me while I allowed myself to finally face the very thing I was always trying to avoid. This was too deep for traditional therapy; I needed to bypass the conscious part of me and get my unconscious and conscious minds to work together so I could resolve this once and for all.

I still remember my first healing session when I muttered the words, "That little girl is safe now."

It took everything in my power to say the word "safe" as I bawled, folded into my lap. I can't even remember how long I cried, but I could feel the tears' energetic hold on me. It was exhausting and peaceful at the same time. It was as if the word "safe" was foreign to me, as if I had never spoken the word in my life.

In a matter of minutes, my chronic back pain had gone away, and in a matter of weeks, I released phobias and traumas and healed old wounds that kept me from living life as intended. This experience was a journey of healing that eventually turned into my purpose. As my healing took place, so did my journey to become a life coach and practitioner of Neuro-Linguistic Programming so that I could help people reframe their perspective on things, break through their pain, and go from surviving to thriving, as intended.

I want you to understand something. This was my life and yes, it was hard but only because I didn't have the awareness that I have today. If I can serve you in any way by showing you how to lean into the discomfort now before things get worse, then I feel that I have fulfilled my purpose in this book. It doesn't have to be hard!

Does the thought of change scare you? You're not alone!

- It made me feel:
- Angry
- Scared
- Defensive
- Insecure
- Resentful
- Inpatient
- Guilt
- Shame
- Blame

In my experience, quick and easy ways of achieving usually don't stick for long. We are not taught how to navigate fear so it's only natural that you would run away from the opportunity of change.

Change comes from within and unless you understand why you are resistant to change and how to move through it, you will find yourself right where you started. In order for things to get better, you have to begin to entertain the thought beneath the resistance and lean into it.

Awareness of my resistance to change was the first step to healing.

The moment you begin to think about change is the moment you have begun the process to change.

FINDING THE SOLUTIONS TO YOUR PROBLEMS:

1) Give yourself permission to let go of the belief that you can't handle or do hard things.

2) We are always doing the best we can with what we know at any given moment, so forgive yourself if you've been holding onto something that you felt you shouldn't have done.

3) Find your proof of success! Where in your life can you find examples of when you faced your fears, struggles, or hurts and were better off as a result?

4) Practice gratitude. We are always learning (even in the hard times). Write a list of the things that you feel grateful for as a result of your experiences.

It's okay to feel uncomfortable. It's part of the process we go through when we evolve, learn, and grow. Allow yourself to be supported. Find guidance and be open to how things could be done differently.

Here's my secret to creating different results if something isn't working: I create a new habit of doing the opposite of whatever has been causing the problem so that I get a different result or outcome. Try it out!

CHAPTER NINE

THE COURAGE OF ODD SOCKS

*"Embrace the magic! It's there,
even when shrouded in chaos and
uncertainty."*

Ruth Fae

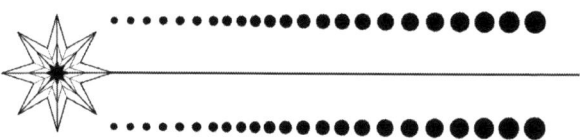

www.faebloodpublications.com.au

Fb: ruth.faewriter
Ig: ruth_fae_writer
Tiktok: ruthfaewriter
LinkedIn: linkedin.com/in/ruth-fae
Goodreads:
goodreads.com/user/show/162791403-ruth-fae

Ruth Fae

Ruth Fae is an intuitive writing coach and editor, best-selling author, and youth mentor. A believer in the unlimited potential of co-creation, she works in energetic flow with her clients to break through their writing blocks, release their stories from their heads and hearts, and confidently share their message with the world.

Through her years as a journalist and copywriter, Ruth has learned that the true magic of storytelling is to heal, nurture, and create connection through sharing the wisdom of our experiences. A rebel at heart, she loves to challenge convention as a coach, speaker, and mentor within the world of indie publishing.

An avid lover of the performing arts, Ruth is a columnist, reviewer, and editor for *Dance Writer Australia*. With a keen interest in encouraging the voice of our younger generations, Ruth values her years of experience writing for *Indigo,* an empowering, unique magazine for teenage girls.

Residing in Melbourne, Australia, Ruth Fae shares her "Life of Love and Magic" with her partner, their blended family of seven children, and an adorably naughty puppy named Merlin.

By my tenth birthday, I'd been the "new kid" at four primary schools across three countries. While following my dad around the world may sound exciting, in reality, constantly adapting to new environments was exhausting. I now understand that this repeated experience caused "little me" to develop a deep need to fit in, a strong desire to belong; it eventually silenced my once strong, outspoken, and somewhat rebellious inherent voice. Outwardly a "good girl" who did what she was asked, made sure everyone else was happy, and never wanted to "be seen" (let alone be seen as different), my (hidden-under-my-mattress) stories displayed my longing to escape the constraints of the double life I lived. By my early teens, "book-nerd-Ruth" dressed as I was expected to, behaved as I was expected to, studied hard at school, and did my best to be "perfect." Wear non-matching socks? No way! Unintentionally, this became an edict I lived by for the next forty years.

My mid-to-late teens were a different story. To my parents, teachers, and most of my peers, I continued to be quiet, studious, and relatively unseen. But the internal screams became louder, and my silenced voice expressed itself through my actions. Like so many of us, I lived the life typical of a 1980s Aussie teen—alcohol, cigarettes, sex, and lies became a regular part of my weekends. My close friends knew "party me," but my parents had no idea and, for the most part, I managed to do enough homework to do well academically and maintain the façade to my teachers. At school, although I believe I was generally well-liked, I remained a "dork," a "nerd," someone to be glossed over and dismissed.

The 1980s are often romantically viewed as a time of freedom. A couple of years ago, my son (also a rebel at heart) expressed that he wished he had been a teenager then—when parents weren't as involved, *Life360* didn't exist, and social media didn't document every part of our lives. He was attracted to the perceived lure of anonymity and independence. As was I. But this was a life of contradictions. The "good girl" and the "rebel" clashed constantly in my head and heart, while my clothes and actions mirrored my struggle to be two different people at the same time. A tightly monitored private school uniform during the week combined with *"No daughter of mine wears black. Only sluts wear black,"* as decreed by my control-freak father, led to fifteen-year-old me buying a tight black crop-top with my first pay, then sneaking it out of the house to wear to the beach or house parties when my parents thought I was sleeping over at a friend's. Our friends were our everything—we backed each other's fibs, collaborated to do whatever we wanted to do, and lived for the weekends and school holidays when we were free to ride our bikes from house to house, laze on the beach, and go to parties wherever they popped up. Yes, there was an inherent, wonderful freedom in this disconnection from our parents and ingrained societal expectations, but this also meant that we handled everything ourselves—sometimes with unexpected and dire consequences.

Back then, mental health wasn't openly discussed. As teens, and even through our twenties, the majority of us had no words for and no understanding of anxiety, depression, abuse, and all their iterations. We knew Scott's dad "bashed him," suspected Issy's step-dad of abusing her, guessed that the reason Sarah drank to blackout every weekend was to escape from something that tortured her psyche. But no one talked about it. And we certainly never told our parents. Every weekend for a few months, my friends and I talked Scott down as, high or drunk, he threatened to end his life. We made sure Issy stayed at our houses rather than having sleepovers at her place, and took turns watching over Sarah to make sure she didn't vomit in her sleep. But we rarely explored our real problems—the internal struggles, deep pain, confusion, sick feelings in our stomachs, sweaty palms and bodies, the abuse we experienced, or the voices that clamored in our heads. What we now know as anxiety was handled with Saturday night stupidity and often dangerous situations that eventuated under a collective veneer of bravado. As tight as we were as friends, hiding our truths from each other and, more importantly, from ourselves had a marked effect that, for so many of my generation, took years to recognize. But times have definitely changed.

Over the past three decades, communication, connection, and awareness have grown exponentially and, thankfully, the youth of today are significantly more self-aware, and way more accepting than I believe we ever were. Mental health, abuse, neglect, abandonment, and the myriad of issues faced by young people are now openly discussed. Now, all this "stuff" is acknowledged and talked about.

In so many ways, the world I grew up in is nothing like the one my children inhabit. It continues to astound me how teens navigate their busy, active, day-to-day lives, on top of their TikTok, Insta, Snapchat, BeReal, and countless other circles of techy-connection. So many group chats, photos, messages, and constant updates from school, dance, sports, and work friends, not to mention the "randoms" they frequently pick up. It amazes me how they keep up with it all—but keep up they do! It's second nature by now, and there's no point denying that technology has had a massive, although not-yet-understood, impact on our youth.

My four children are now aged twelve to twenty-one. Guiding them through their lives so far, I've come to realize that, even though the world is a very different place, navigating familial and societal expectations, puberty, friendships, alcohol, drugs, sexuality, and technology remains a significant challenge passed on from generation to generation.

As a parent, I've tried (sometimes desperately) to give my children what I didn't have. Stability, connection to the wider community, and the freedom to talk to me about anything they choose, no matter what it may be. Together, we're navigating their mental and physical health issues, the effects of the pandemic, school, friendships, and relationships, plus the odd foray into "not so good" choices. But ultimately, they are young people with fears, needs, and dreams, and there are certainly times when life does not go as planned.

Today's youth are amazing. The young people who have flowed in and out of my house, work, and community for the past twenty years are so much more self-aware than we were in the '80s; they openly question and challenge their identities and how they "fit" into the world around them. And if they don't fit, they fight to find their place. The ever-growing awareness being brought to the importance of mental health has given them the words and permission to talk more openly about their feelings and experiences—but, sadly, abuse remains prevalent in our society and kids are still being hurt. They still struggle. And they deserve support.

Mid-pandemic, I sat with a young woman who was going through a very difficult time in her life. In the midst of world-wide upheaval, she was dealing with a chaos of her own: the breakdown of family relationships, significant mental health issues including severe anxiety and depression, and the effects of a series of traumatic events. Challenged on all levels, she was struggling to cope with and understand how this was manifesting in her life, her body, and her emotional landscape.

That afternoon in the park, as we observed the strangeness of the lockdown-induced empty playground, we talked. Not parent-to-child or mentor-to-youth but person-to-person, we explored how life events have impacted us physically and emotionally and how they have altered our inherent beliefs and behaviors. This conversation was eye-opening; at eighteen years old, she showed such bravery, maturity, and self-awareness. We talked about using mindfulness, breathing, and "being in the moment" techniques to deal with anxiety and panic attacks. She explained some of the tools she learned as part of the Dialectical Behaviour Therapy (DBT) course she had just completed to help manage her symptoms. I was mind-blown—barely an adult, she had a huge amount of knowledge and understanding about mental health; at her age, I didn't even know words like "emotional regulation" existed! But what struck me so strongly about this conversation is that this brave young woman is "doing the work" now, rather than waiting until she's older, when negative beliefs and behaviors could become even more entrenched in her psyche and much harder to shift. Learning these valuable skills now will certainly help her navigate her path through life. Even when the road gets bumpy, she will have tools and inner knowledge to support her.

To understand how your mind and body work in connection with each other is so valuable. To learn to establish your boundaries, understand your reactions to other people and events, and see yourself as the amazing, unique person you are is the greatest gift you can give yourself.

Shit does happen. And the resulting trauma can feel horrible; it's scary, painful, and often dangerous. Things people say or do to us can dim the beautiful light we are all born with. But there are tools, techniques, and skills you can learn to give you strength and agency and reduce the compounding effects of trauma that may negatively affect your future. Young people who do choose to speak up, seek help, and fight for their rightful place as valid, dynamic humans show such bravery.

As a teen, I was afraid a lot of the time. Afraid of my parents, of losing friends and, most of all, afraid of not being allowed a voice. There were no words to describe my deepest fears and emotions. I'm sure there are times you feel that way, too. But I can see from my kids and their friends (not to mention TikTok), that your generation is learning from the mistakes of your parents' and previous generations. You have greater awareness. You embrace diversity and are open to change. You are aware of the value of communication, connection, and therapy. And, thankfully, you now have the language to express yourselves with greater clarity, to use your voices, to be seen and heard. I urge you to keep speaking up and fighting for yourselves—be courageous, shine your light, and follow your dreams, even when it feels difficult or scary.

Having support to shine that light as you navigate your school years and beyond is super important. Who do you turn to when you need advice or someone to simply listen to you? Siblings, parents, your best friend? A sports coach, aunt, or uncle? Maybe a teacher, well-being counselor, or a friend's parent? My relationship with my parents was never easy but after I met her when I was fourteen, my best friend's mum became a wonderful support for many years, even after I had my own children. Non-judgemental and way more in touch with teenagers than my mum and dad, Helen was a safe space, a warm hug, and an open heart. No matter what was happening in my life, she was someone I could trust.

Recently, I spoke to a clinical psychologist who specializes in working with young people. She explained that there are currently a number of studies exploring trust, particularly in relation to the experience of youth during the COVID-19 pandemic. Basically, the fear and lack of control we all experienced as a result of government-enforced lockdowns and restrictions has had a significant negative impact on who young people feel they can trust. According to her research, the constantly changing "rules," lack of freedom, separation from friends and extended family, and incessant influx of sometimes contradictory information through the media have created a collective distrust of authority figures such as politicians, teachers, doctors, and parents and other adults. Even some primary school-aged children showed distinct lack of trust in their teachers and parents, simply from not knowing whether they would be at school from one day to the next.

Lack of trust leads to feelings of anger, disappointment, suspicion, betrayal or abandonment, and self-doubt—totally not ideal for the growing, developing minds and bodies of our youth. As a result, psychologists and other medical professionals are seeing a marked increase in general and social anxiety and depression in young people since the pandemic began. They are also increasingly turning to each other, and to social media, to find the answers, comfort, and connection they desperately desire.

There is nothing wrong with talking to your friends about the issues that worry or hurt you. But sometimes you or your friends may face problems that are too big. When I was fifteen, one of my school friends told me about abuse she was experiencing at home. While we weren't close friends, she was also struggling with the dynamics of her friendship group at the time, so she talked to me. But it was far too much for me to handle. Terribly worried and on the verge of tears, I didn't know what to say or how to help her. Sure, I listened and gave her a big hug, but she told me she was suicidal—what was I supposed to do? Tell a teacher? Ring the police? Talk to my mum (who would probably just ring the school anyway)? How could I betray her confidence? For a week, I lived in fear that she simply wouldn't turn up to school one day; I believed that if something terrible happened to her, it would be my fault because I didn't do anything to help her. She was suffering. I was under immense pressure. None of this was healthy, or safe, for either of us.

Thankfully, my amazing English literature teacher recognized there was something worrying me and called me in for what is now known as a "well-being check." Crying and scared, eventually I told her what was going on, and she took the problem out of my hands. To be honest, I'm not entirely sure what happened because my friend never spoke to me about it again (and she left the school at the end of the year), but I do know that her mum rang mine a few weeks later to say thank you for my bravery in speaking up when her daughter couldn't.

My point here is two-fold. It's so hard to deal with problems on our own, particularly when they are big and overwhelming. Humans simply aren't built that way. We need connection, support, and love to feel safe and happy. As you grow up, your friendships will often give you this sense of belonging and understanding; you trust your friends to "get" you when it feels like so many other people don't. But what do you do when the problems are bigger, more complex, or more serious than you, and your friends, can handle? And if you are questioning your trust in your parents, teachers, and wider community, where do you turn for support in this fast-paced, technology-driven, ever-changing world?

When my kids were little people, I was concerned that they wouldn't always want to talk to me about their problems. My childhood was so unstable and lacking in trust that I often felt lonely, unseen, and unsupported. I simply didn't have siblings or adults I could easily talk to about my worries, fears, and problems—and I know that affected me greatly as an adult. So, determined my kids would not experience their childhood in this way, periodically I played "Who Can You Trust" with them. We drew around our hands and wrote the names of five people (other than their dad and me) who they could talk to if they needed help or advice. As they matured, the names on their "hands" changed, and they started to discern that they could go to different people for different problems.

There is validity to this thought process. *Who are five people (other than your friends) you could trust when you are struggling with a problem or decision?* It is super helpful to identify these people before you become overwhelmed with pain, fear, or anxiety; it can be hard to think straight when you're suffering. But if you've identified them beforehand, and know they are safe, just like Helen was for me, then you always have somewhere to go when you hit a bump in your road.

A couple of years ago, I was scared to face a difficult situation in my life. I knew I had to speak up for the sake of myself and other people, but confrontation still didn't come easily to me. So I met with a friend to work through the issue and figure out what to say and how to say it. I felt sick in my guts, nervous, anxious, and struggled to feel brave. I didn't trust myself to find the right words. He suggested that, when the time came, I wear something to remind me of my courage in speaking up—a shirt or piece of jewelry that would help me to keep going when my fear felt overwhelming.

A picture flashed into my mind of my daughter when she was four years old. She loved wearing bright, flamboyant clothes, colors and patterns all mixed together, totally defying convention. And every day, she wore non-matching socks! At the time, I loved it—mainly because I saw her as the epitome of everything I couldn't be as a child. She was brave, determined, and didn't care what other people thought; her clothes were a form of self-expression, and they made her happy! So on the day of the confrontation, I intentionally wore non-matching socks.

It felt strange, but they did make me smile on the inside. They symbolized my courage in taking the risk to finally find my voice, speak up, and be seen as me. When my conversation faltered and my brain yelled at me to back away, I looked down at my feet, at the different colors poking from the top of my sneakers, and, strange as it may sound, my socks gave me the strength I needed to continue.

Sarah, Scott, and Issy are all doing okay, and Helen is, thankfully, still passing down her love and wisdom to her grandson and his friends. I'm settled, happy, and no longer feel the need to scream, internally or otherwise. What I have learned since those rebellious teenage years is that we all have value and worth, and we all deserve to be seen and heard. It's why I do the work I do, and why I am so driven to advocate for you, our youth, to speak up and voice your truths, share your ideas, and be supported to create change.

Our world isn't always the kindest place to be, but there is magic to be found, even when it's hiding in chaos and uncertainty. Look for that magic, embrace love and happiness, and, when life inevitably does send challenges your way, make the choice to ask for help and guidance from people you trust. Love yourself enough to "do the work" to keep yourself mentally and physically healthy. And even when you doubt it, your "odd socks" are there to remind you that you carry the strength and courage to step out into that world and experience life your way.

WHO CAN YOU TRUST?

You don't have to handle everything yourself! When problems feel overwhelming, it often helps to talk to someone who cares about you. But sometimes it can be hard to speak to your parents, especially if the problem involves them. *So, who can you talk to? Who do you trust?*

This will change as you mature, and the best person to give you help and advice may vary, depending on the problem you face. It can be helpful to do this quick activity whenever an issue or decision you're not sure about comes up in your life.

Who are five people (other than your friends) you can trust when you are struggling with a problem or decision?

Draw around your hand (as you get older, or better at practicing this, you can do it in your mind).

In each finger, write a person you feel safe and comfortable to share your worries with. This may be a:

- Teacher
- Coach
- Aunt or Uncle
- Friend's parent
- Adult family friend
- Grandparent
- Older brother or sister
- School well-being person
- Youth Group leader
- Minister or Leader of your Church, Temple or Synagogue
- Doctor
- Policeman/woman
- Help Line - many youth services have text options if you don't feel comfortable talking on the phone

Then, ask these five people if they are happy to be a person you can talk to, or message, if you need them.

Make sure you have their phone numbers or email addresses so it's easy to contact them.

It can be hard to think straight when you're suffering, so it's super helpful to identify these people before you become overwhelmed with pain, fear, or anxiety. When you know who these five trusted people are, you always have a safe space to go.

Chapter ten

Become Your Own Best Friend

"The things we miss out on can still be gained. This time, by us."

Stephanie Burgess

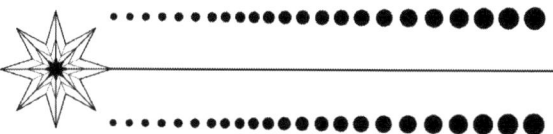

fb: inhaleigniteyoga
ig: stephaniebcoaching

Stephanie Burgess

Stephanie Burgess knew from a very young age that she was meant to make a difference. She is intuitive, self-aware, and an eternal optimist. In 2020, Stephanie left her twenty-year career in wealth management to pursue her dream of making an impact and becoming an entrepreneur in the wellness industry. Her studies in health and fitness, yoga, and empowerment coaching have provided her with a well-rounded and deep foundation as a coach and movement instructor.

Stephanie naturally gravitates to supporting and empowering those around her. She has always had the ability to see the best in people, with the understanding and belief that absolutely every human is filled with potential and possibility. Growing up, Stephanie was able to accept her environment for what it was, take the experience and learnings, and use them as motivation for her future.

Stephanie lives just outside of Toronto, Ontario, where she is raising an empowered daughter and creating opportunities to reach others on a deeper level.

For most of my life, I have felt out of place, different, like I didn't fit in. The things I thought and worried about when I was young were not the same things my friends were dealing with. I usually kept to myself in my own little bubble, showing just enough of myself to get by and keeping everything else hidden inside. The truth was, I felt embarrassed. I felt ashamed. You might say I felt really cringe. I felt as though I lived a very different life from the friends and schoolmates around me. I would watch the other girls my age with their friends and family and wonder what it felt like to have a "normal" connection, to have a bond with their parents: to be fully supported, to be seen and heard, comforted and encouraged. To have emotional stability.

My family moved a lot, which was super hard on a kid trying to find self-esteem and acceptance in a big world. New neighborhoods, new schools, and having to yet again be the new kid really didn't bring any sense of stability to my life. This was on top of a home that was already unstable and filled with uncertainty and chaos, where alcoholism and lack of emotional support were part of the parenting I received.

My parents split up when I was around seven years old. Looking back, it's a bit of a blur, but I do know that instability and insecurity made up my foundation. I was always walking on eggshells, waiting for the next thing to happen. Closeness and bonding didn't exist in my world, and at a young age, I learned that the only person I could really trust and count on was me. I learned that if I wanted or needed something, it would be up to me to figure it out.

Although I developed really unhelpful beliefs and became completely disconnected from who I was, I somehow also knew that this reality didn't have to be my future. Somehow, I already knew that I could choose to do things differently—and that I would. I couldn't wait to grow up and become an adult so I could create the life I desperately wanted. Much of my time was spent daydreaming about the kind of home I would live in, where I would work, and how I would feel. A life filled with love, acceptance, stability, and abundance. Everything I dreamed of as a child, I would make mine.

Part of me is sad that I wished my childhood away. If you are currently doing the same, I get it. The other part of me is thankful and super proud that I had this inner drive and knowing from such a young age because it is undoubtedly what projected me into adulthood.

As an adult, and after doing a lot of personal work, I now have awareness of the beliefs carried with me from my childhood: beliefs of unworthiness and rejection. Developing this awareness is probably one of the biggest exercises we can do to grow as humans. I really encourage you to start doing this as soon as you can. Raise awareness around everything. Be curious and ask yourself questions. To expand my knowledge and grow as a human has been so empowering, and it will be for you, too. The sooner you begin to build these skills, the sooner you begin to navigate life a bit better.

It wasn't until I began to open myself to new opportunities and people that I learned about the world and myself. In the beginning, it was really uncomfortable to stretch myself and try new things. I didn't like change at all and usually stuck to what I knew and what felt comfortable. I read a lot of personal growth books, listened to podcasts, watched documentaries, and jumped into different training and certification programs that interested me.

Growth is definitely hidden in discomfort. I began to make connections about how my past experiences and environment had created the reality I was living as an adult. Diving into this work introduced me to the concept of consciousness. I was literally walking around completely unaware of myself and my surroundings, like living under a rock or in a fog. Better late than never—learning about consciousness became the starting point to finding out who I really was. Who I was outside of everything I had been told and trained to believe. This was the start of the rest of my life.

We are raised in a world filled with so many layers of conditioning. There are beliefs everywhere that we automatically assume to be true. We typically aren't raised to question these beliefs; we are just expected to accept them. We aren't always raised to understand who we are or to believe in ourselves. We aren't guided to uncover what we really want or what lights us up from the inside out. But these are exactly the things that make us so fascinating and unique. Instead, we are taught to follow the traditions and milestones that have always been. To find the labels that describe us, and then to work within the confines of that box. To walk through life without a clue about who we really are, why we are here, and how much possibility exists. We grow up and follow the sequence of events we are told we are "supposed to do" without ever really asking ourselves what it is that we want. What is true for us? Do I even want that? We become disconnected from ourselves and life as we repeat each day on cruise control without ever realizing it.

I will tell you, though, once we experience a taste of what it's like to wake up . . . a whole other world opens up for us.

I'm going to share with you the first keys that began to open up my world. How I have managed to overcome my crappy childhood experiences and the stress I felt as a youth. How I have built confidence and self-trust, managed anxiety, regulated my emotions, and literally changed the course of my life. These are the first things I did along my path to unlearning and learning what is meaningful for me.

Everything we don't receive as a child or during the years of youth is never lost. In fact, the things we long for, the gaps that remain, can always be recovered and filled. This time, by us. As we step into acceptance of all the experiences that have made us who we are, we can also claim responsibility for what we do next with what we have. It's truly up to us. Cycles continue until someone can stand up and be the one who breaks the pattern. Someone who decides to become their own hero.

Sometimes when we are hurting, it's easier to blame other people, especially the people who were responsible for us. I certainly did when I was younger. Sadly, though, all this does is keep us from stepping into our own power. The truth is that our parents, our teachers, our coaches, and everyone around us are also growing and learning in their own way. They are not perfect. I truly believe that people do the best they can with what they have. You only know what you know; you don't know what you were never taught. This can be such a freeing realization. It allows us to move toward acceptance of what was and acceptance of responsibility for what happens next. Once we understand this and begin to see people and situations from a different perspective, we are able to find compassion and acceptance for who they are, and also for ourselves. This doesn't mean that we automatically forgive those who have hurt us. It just means that we begin to look at things differently, which opens the door to healing our wounds.

My advice to you is to become your own best friend—not in an isolated, anti-social way but in an "I trust myself and my voice the most" kind of way. Shift your focus from what's outside of you to what's inside of you. It is so important that our own voice is the strongest and most important force in our lives. Being guided from a place within allows us to understand and honor what is true for us. Listening to our own voice and gut takes us down our unique individual path instead of the road other people think we should take. We then begin to build a strong foundation of self-trust and an inner compass that will guide us for the rest of our lives. When we are led by this place, we know exactly who we are and what we want and we have the confidence to create a meaningful life.

When we become our own best friend, we become unstoppable in all areas of life. Everything we need, we are able to first and foremost give to ourselves. You may be surprised at the simplicity at the steps I am about to share with you. I sure doubted that these basic practices would change my life. Thousands of dollars and certifications later, it turns out that these things were right under my nose. Now I am sharing them with you so that you have the head start I didn't have. Sometimes it's the smallest things that are the most impactful.

Step One:

Slow down and get comfortable being uncomfortable in still-ness . . . and YES, if this is new for you, it will be super uncomfortable! Slowing down allows you to become present in the NOW, in this very moment and in your current experience. When you allow yourself to be in this space, you have no other option but to face whatever is coming up for you. That itch, that thought, that discomfort—this is where you have the chance to sit with yourself and just notice. It's in this place where you begin to connect to your breath, body, and thoughts. This place scares many people, and it wasn't the most comfortable for me in the beginning either, but I promise you, it changed everything. It's also important to do this practice with compassion and kindness for yourself. Just sit with yourself and take note of what you notice. Allow yourself to become curious about what comes up. Thoughts will likely be popping through your head at an alarming rate. This is normal. All you need to do is be aware of the thought and then let it go. The richest nuggets are in these moments. Take even just a couple minutes a day to just sit in a quiet place and be with yourself. Remember—you are not here to judge your experience, just to be in it.

Step Two:

Learn to breathe. One of the BEST tools I have come to rely on is my breath. I know . . . we all breathe. What's the big deal, right? Everyone breathes, yes, but do we breathe fully and consciously? Most of us don't. So the next practice I recommend is observing your breath. Start by just noticing how you are breathing. Don't change a thing; just become aware. Is your breathing fast or is it slow? Are your breaths shallow or are they deeper? Where do you feel your breath in your body? Can you sense the temperature of the air on the way in and on the way out? As time goes on, practice breathing with deeper and fuller breaths. It may feel difficult at first (it definitely was for me!), but I promise you that the more you do this, the easier it will become. Practice while sitting in traffic or while studying. The beauty is that you can do this anywhere, anytime. Breathing on purpose widens the window of both patience and tolerance. It brings focus, and it also is a great way to bring yourself into the present moment! When you can sit with yourself and your breath, you are priming yourself to handle discomfort and to be able to calm yourself when needed. Life is so full of ups and downs, and being able to navigate how we respond and feel is so important. Soothing yourself is a life skill we should all have in our pocket.

Step Three:

The check-in. So now that you have begun to slow down and breathe a little more deeply, I am going to share with you my FAVORITE practice! In our day-to-day lives, it is so easy to become wrapped up in our roles, responsibilities, and tasks. We jump from one thing to the next without a thought, constantly checking email and social media and never really allowing any space for personal reflection.

The check-in is simply finding stillness (which you know about), closing your eyes (to minimize distractions), and focusing on your breath. See, you are already halfway there! You've got this! Once you are feeling settled, begin to relax all the parts of your body. Soften your eyelids, relax your jaw, drop your shoulders down away from your ears. Relax your chest and belly so that your breath flows effortlessly. Notice what is happening in your body. Are you holding any tension or tightness? Is there something that you have been ignoring that could really use some attention? What is your body signaling to you?

Then begin to observe your thoughts. Just be curious here; remember—no judgment! Is your mind a little more active? (If it is, that's okay!!) Stay with your breath. Are you noticing that it is difficult to slow the train of thoughts? (Again, it's okay!) What kinds of thoughts are they? Observing your thoughts is a life-changing practice. Not everything we think is true—in fact, most of it isn't—so this is a great way to notice the types of messages you have running through your mind.

Next, ask yourself a super important question: "What do I need?" I don't mean "you" as a student, a spouse, a parent, a sibling, an employee, or a friend. I mean YOU. Just you, as a human being, without any titles or labels. I need you to come back to the core of who you are with this question. You can ask yourself as many times as needed, and then allow some silence and stillness to see what bubbles up. It could be as simple as "I need to drink more water" or it can be something else, like "I need to step away from this person because they stress me out." Whatever comes up is okay. There is no right or wrong.

Whatever does come up for you, though—I want you to treat it like gold. The whole point of this practice is to honor yourself, so letting the message float away won't be helpful. Your next step will be to act on whatever it is that you need. This is the part where you take action. Acting based on your needs builds self-trust. Depending on what came up for you, this can also be a moment when you realize a little more work is involved. For example, what you need might also be something that really makes you feel anxious or nervous about moving forward. This is a great awareness to have, and it's absolutely okay to be nervous or anxious or whatever else you are feeling about taking a new step. Remember that growth is often paired with discomfort, and this is it! Use your breathing and spend some time soothing yourself around whatever is coming up for you. You can move your body, try tapping, dance it out, take a walk—find whatever works for you.

Especially in the early days of this practice, you may not get any answers, and that's okay, too! At first, I was SO disconnected from myself, but in time, the messages came. It felt good to access these learnings. There is nothing like feeling good about who you are and your ability to navigate whatever life throws at you.

Your new life starts now, and I will be cheering you on every single step of the way. You are brilliant, you are worthy, and regardless of how you started in life, there is still space and possibility to create everything you have ever imagined.

XO

HOW TO PRACTICE THE CHECK IN

Step One:

Close your eyes and focus on your breathing. Breathe softly into your belly.

Step Two:

Relax your face, shoulders, chest, and stomach. Notice what you are feeling in your body. Do your best to relax any tension.

Step Three:

Ask yourself, "What do I need?" Allow yourself to sit with this question in silence.

Step Four:

Pay attention to what bubbles up. There is no right or wrong answer. Whatever comes up for you is what's meant for you.

Step Five:

Honor the message. Give yourself whatever it is you are needing. This is where self-trust is built.

CHAPTER ELEVEN

THROWING A FORK IN THE WHEEL OF DEPRESSION

"Grab your fork and throw it: You can stop the spinning wheel of depression!"

Heather Marie Spitzer

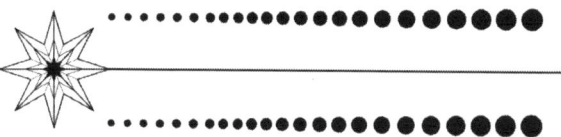

www.rebelheartscoaching.com

Fb: rebelheartscoaching
Ig: rebelheartscoaching
Tiktok: rebelheartscoaching
Youtube: rebelheartscoaching

Heather Marie Spitzer

Heather Spitzer of Rebel Hearts Coaching LLC is a certified integrative and wellness life coach and a soul-coaching oracle card reader whose passion is to help those on their healing journey to overcome the grip of depression so they can live their best life. Having spent well over 20 years in severe depression herself, she understands the depths of depression and its iron grip on life.

It took extreme circumstances to make Heather question her beliefs about herself and choose to finally start loving herself. In doing so, she started to ask herself what she wanted in life. As she explored this new way of being, she began to make some pretty radical changes.

It took many baby steps over a period of time to finally break the iron grip depression held on her life, but Heather now enjoys creating a life she loves! She finds no greater honor than being a light in someone's darkness to help them find and embrace their own inner light, their wisdom, and that Rebel Heart to act as their life's compass.

At age fifteen, my life turned completely upside down. We had just moved from Germany to Georgia, US after the Gulf War, which my dad had fought in. He didn't come back from the war the same, but we thought he would find his new normal with time and all would be okay. That wasn't the case. It wasn't even a year after coming back that he died of suicide. My last words to him were, "Screw you!" Talk about a burden of guilt with that one.

I couldn't cope. I barely functioned. I went through the mandatory motions as best I could, but it wasn't long before thoughts of suicide crept into my own mind. I just wanted the pain to stop. I told Mom about my thoughts, and it didn't go over very well. Inpatient psychiatric care was on the table now, and that freaked me out! So I didn't say anything anymore. Nothing that would give insights into the depths of my emotions, into my pain.

Mom eventually got me into counseling as my world just got darker and darker. I went on "happy pills" and tried to work through things in counseling, but at this point I already believed that sharing my innermost thoughts and feelings was dangerous. It would get me into trouble or get me locked in the "looney bin." Either way, talking about my emotions didn't feel safe. Facing them didn't feel safe either. I was terrified. Terrified of my own emotions; terrified of people's responses to my emotions; terrified that I'd be locked up in a padded room if they saw too much of what I was feeling. So I shoved the feels down as deep as they'd go.

The more I buried my emotions, covered them up, pretended, and hid from them, the more intense the depression became. Even on medication, I still thought frequently of suicide. Then I'd feel guilt and shame over: how could I think like that knowing how I felt from Dad's suicide?! How could I cause Mom and my younger brother more pain by my "selfishness?" How could I BE so selfish?!

The inner turmoil built up to a point where I was melting down and lashing out frequently. Told to clean my room? Fine! I would rake my arms across my dusty dresser, flinging everything into the wall, screaming at the injustice of it all. Time to clean the bathroom? Fine! Comet would fly everywhere as I crumbled to the floor sobbing, barely able to breathe for the Comet dust in the air.

The most simple things became difficult. Watching *Lion King* for the first time? Oh, dear lord, sob fest in the theater when Mufasa died. English teacher talking about how people who die of suicide and leave a note don't really want to die (Dad left a note)? That was a dead run into the bathroom to let the boogers fly.

I didn't know the first thing about honoring my emotions. It didn't feel like I could truly talk to anyone. I didn't even like talking to myself—that was usually ugly! In all actuality, I just didn't want to feel. I felt utterly alone and completely overwhelmed.

Here's what I wish I had known and had experienced through this season:

- I wish I had known that emotions weren't evil, and they didn't have to be fought against. I couldn't see how damaging suppressing my emotions was to myself and to others, or how my beliefs about myself were keeping me stuck in my downward depression spiral.
- I wish I had experienced an emotionally safe space at home where I wasn't upsetting others or experiencing others' fearful or angry responses.

Eventually, the painful emotions got too hard to handle. I knew I hurt—a lot. I knew part of me just wanted to die, but I also knew that I couldn't leave Mom and my brother like that. Whenever I would get to that point of feeling suicidal and would start to dream about it, the guilt and shame would wash over me like a waterfall of hot tar. I felt stuck, I hurt beyond words, and I couldn't speak. In my mind, I couldn't ask anyone else for help, but I needed some way to make those thoughts go away. So instead of ending it all, I started cutting instead.

One day, I was sitting there on my floor, lost in my own hell, and I happened to spot my Swiss Army knife. I started fiddling with it and wondering what kind of pressure it would actually take to create a fatal wound. I couldn't do it, not really, but that didn't stop me from thinking about it. With my knife in hand, I opened one of the blades, testing its sharpness (Dad taught us well to keep a blade's edge well-honed in case we had to skin a squirrel to survive in the woods!). Yep, it was sharp enough to do some serious damage.

I started to cut in places no one would see, the areas that stayed covered even if I was in a swimsuit. It was a strange sensation to feel such heaviness of emotion, hold such dark thoughts, and feel my skin cut and the blood begin to ooze out. It's a crazy place to be. It's like that cut somehow let my pain come out through my blood. Definitely NOT a healthy way to deal with things! Sadly, I carried this pattern with me through my late thirties.

Eventually, Mom found out. This was the second time that inpatient psychiatric care jumped on the table as a very imminent option to get me help. What I didn't know then was that no amount of inpatient care at that stage would have done much of anything because I was blind to the root of my problem.

That root: I hated myself. No medication, no treatment, no counseling or behavior modification could have changed that in me. I had to reach a point in life where I CHOSE to love myself instead. Then, and only then, could I truly heal from all I held within. I wish I could say this happened early in life, but alas . . . I am stubborn!

What I wish I had known and had experienced through this season:

- I wish I had recognized and known that there were always options for help. Sadly, I wasn't able to see that there really were ways out of this.

- I wish I had experienced being held tightly in Mom's arms as she told me that everything would be okay, that cutting wasn't a solution to my pain. I wish I was able to experience her love that wasn't overshadowed by her fear.

Jump ahead a number of years. I'm now twenty-four and married (my second time) with three baby boys. I still didn't care much about myself, but now *I* was Mom. My life wasn't all about *me* anymore.

One night when the boys were upstairs asleep, my husband and I got into a fight. It got ugly, and I was tossed around like a rag doll. I had experienced abuse before but not quite like this. The experience left me feeling worthless and weak. I felt all those dark things from when I was fifteen burst forth again. It was almost like my brain quit working altogether this time, though.

I was hurting so badly, physically and emotionally, and I was back in that space of not being able to handle it. I had no conscious thought of killing myself, but there I was with a blade in hand. Due to my biology nerd schooling, I knew anatomy well at this point and knew the lethal swipe to take, so I did. Twice.

I was left with barely two scratches and feeling so confused. It should have worked! Plenty sharp enough and plenty of pressure applied, so why didn't it work? All of a sudden, it was like my brain engaged again, and I thought of my boys sleeping upstairs.

I collapsed in heaving sobs. *"How could I do that?! How selfish am I?! How could he do this to me?!"* The thoughts went on and on. The guilt and shame I felt were truly beyond words. I had tried to leave my own kids like Dad left me.

A couple of days later as I was talking to Mom (she's a bit psychic, by the way), she asked me what happened that night. I didn't tell her I had tried to kill myself; I wouldn't. I told her we fought and I got a bit busted up. She said, "No, that's not what I'm talking about." She then said she was going to tell me about her vision and that I was to explain it to her. (How does Mom always know?!)

In her vision, she saw me sitting in a chair with my hands covering my face as I sobbed. Dad was on one side of me and Gramma, who had passed the year following Dad, was on the other. She said they both looked at her and held out their left arms, which had bleeding cuts from their wrist halfway up their arms. They had tears streaming down their faces.

They saved me from myself.

I broke down crying. There was so much to the feels, and I couldn't hold it in anymore. I knew I couldn't keep going like this. Something had to change.

I wish I could say this was the day that I chose to love myself, but it wasn't. I spent years seeking religion and trying to find a savior who could save me from my hell. Even as a ministry leader in a Christian church, I eventually found myself sitting in bed with a gun in my lap, considering my options. It took many years before I finally chose me, before I finally made one simple choice that would change my life forever: the one choice that would put me on the path that would lead me out of depression to create a new life for myself. That one simple choice: to love myself as I had dreamed of being loved—unconditionally.

What I wish I had known and had experienced through this season:

- I wish I had known that salvation was within me; that I was my own savior.
- I wish I had known how powerful I truly was.
- I wish I could have believed in myself and been strong enough to leave an abusive relationship. I couldn't see my own innate worth and I couldn't see that I had a powerful spiritual team just waiting for me to invite their help and allow space for them to do so.

Skip ahead a few (or so) more years. I'm now thirty-nine years old. I'm still in a toxic, abusive marriage and setting horrible examples for my kids about what love and marriage ought to be. I still didn't love myself.

There was another horrible night that saw me curled up in a fetal position, tucked into the corner of my bedroom, being screamed at. When would it end?! I did contemplate suicide again, but thankfully it wasn't as strong of a pull as it once was. Again, I knew I couldn't keep going like this. It had to end.

It became clear that I would have to embark on a healing journey on my own. Mom actually got me started. We went on a road trip together for a family reunion and as we holed up in a hotel room to shower and get some sleep, I burst into tears after checking my phone. I was getting some pretty ugly messages from the husband, and his words cut very deep.

Handing my phone to Mom, I let her see what was being said. She read the messages and then as she handed my phone back, she told me to get my journal. I totally didn't understand, but I did it anyway. She told me to start writing: to write out all the things I believed about myself. I can't say that I had ever really thought about my beliefs before, but I played along.

As I started to write what I believed about myself, I just kept crying. I was shocked (but not shocked) at the things that were coming out. It was awful. This is when Mom told me that I had to choose, and that I had the power of choice. I could choose to continue to believe those awful things, or I could choose new beliefs. Nothing was going to change until I decided to love myself and believe differently.

We then wrote out all the opposites of those beliefs: all the good ones. Instead of "I'm not worthy of the love I long for," it was now "I'm worthy of unconditional love." Instead of "I'm only deserving of death," it was now "I deserve a long, happy, healthy life."

It was a slow process, but it wasn't long before I was divorced and learning how to live life on my own terms. The depression didn't go away miraculously (oh, how I wish!), but it did eventually reach a point where it no longer ruled my life. Each day I spent changing the patterns of my thoughts, my speech, and my daily habits. I committed to choosing "healthy" and "loving" for me.

What I learned in this season:

- I was worthy of the life I longed for. I was worthy of health. I was worthy of love.
- I had help around me that I couldn't see before.
- I was powerful because I could *choose.*

Depression is like this spinning wheel we get stuck in that carries us into dark places. We have to find our "fork" to throw into that wheel so we can learn a new way. My "fork" was to literally tell myself, "Shut the fork up!" when my mind got stuck in that spinning wheel of awful thoughts that trapped me in toxic emotion. I had to consciously speak to myself differently. I memorized that new list of beliefs and repeated it every time my head would get stuck in those deep, dark rabbit holes. I would repeat it like a mantra until my emotions calmed down and I would be reminded that I could live differently.

I reminded myself daily of how lovable and worthy I was, even when I wasn't feeling it. It was really a process of rewiring my brain pathways from the ruts I built on that wheel of depression to new pathways that were being built on love.

I also found the joy of oracle cards. When I didn't have the counselor, the coach, or the spiritual guru to guide me through my own heart, I found that oracle cards were a beautiful way for me to find myself—for myself. Through drawing cards every day, I was able to find encouragement, guidance, and support from within. I felt my sense of confidence grow and my gift of intuition expand. I found a new way of looking at life and new ways of nurturing myself: mind, body, and soul. Oracle cards are a beautiful tool and helped me tremendously in really breaking those chains that held me to that wheel of depression.

Regardless of the tools you find to help you along the way, always remember that the power to throw that fork in the wheel of depression and create a new life experience for yourself is IN YOU! Embrace it!! Throw your fork!! You're worthy, love . . . YOU ARE WORTHY!!!

HOW TO GRAB YOUR FORK AND THROW IT:

Step One:

Believe that you are worthy and capable of creating the change you want! It all starts with making an active choice to see and do things differently.

Step Two:

Ask yourself what you believe about your life/self and start writing out all that comes up; the good, the bad, and the fugly. If you don't like a belief, flip it around, write its opposite, and create a mantra. Repeat that mantra whenever your thoughts try to feed the negative. Choose to believe better about and for yourself!

Step Three:

Pay attention to your thoughts and emotions and how they come together. If you feel like garbage, bring awareness to your thoughts. Look at how the thoughts feed the emotion. Recognize the power you DO have in any moment to change your "stinking thinking." Practice feeding the feels you like, versus the ones that keep you in that hole.

Step Four:

Practice, practice, practice! Shifting thoughts and beliefs doesn't happen overnight, but don't let trips make you quit. You are STRONG and AMAZING, and every time you get back up, you're refusing to feed the depression!

In every step you take, practice holding grace and unconditional love for yourself!

CHAPTER TWELVE

HOW MY PARENTS' DIVORCE HELPED ME BECOME THE BEST MOM

"Sharing your emotions is the key to understanding yourself and letting go of the past."

Karen Brunette

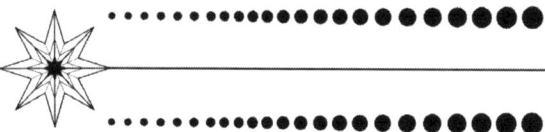

fb: karen.brunnette
ig: karen.brunnette

Karen Brunette

Karen Brunnette grew up in Kingston, Ontario with a love for all things creative. She is a multi-passionate advocate for families who have lived through the challenges of experiencing a traumatic head injury. She has been featured on multiple television programs speaking about the life changes that occur after a serious head trauma. Karen is a dedicated volunteer in the public school system with years of experience on the parent committee and has a vested interest in helping youth live a fulfilling and happy life.

We understand divorce a lot differently today than we used to. Sometimes divorce is a positive change that needs to happen in a family for everyone to get what they need. But back when my parents separated, it took a heavy toll on all of us.

It started when I was nine years old. My parents said they were taking us out for dinner and that when we got home, they wanted to talk to us. I immediately guessed what they wanted to talk about. My mind was swirling. I had two older brothers, but they didn't seem to be worried at all. By the time we got home, I was ready to burst. I walked through the front door and hollered, "You're getting a divorce!" The tears started as the emotion bubbled up—my life totally changed from that day on.

You did not talk about divorce fifty-two years ago. We weren't allowed to tell anyone: not our friends, not our teachers, not anyone. My dad's parents didn't know how to handle the divorce and shunned us. It was so new that they didn't know how to treat us anymore. We hardly ever saw them, and they lived in the area. Eventually, after my parents remarried, my new step-grandparents never treated us the same as their natural grandchildren. No one knew how to have these complex relationships back then.

My dad told us he was moving out, and our beautiful home was going up for sale. Where were we kids and my mom going to live? My dad would not be around every day or night; what were we supposed to do? It would have helped me to feel like I could ask questions and be part of the process so I could understand all of these big feelings I was having.

Our home was sold, and we moved to a house I hated. I didn't know how to accept all these changes, and I felt upset in my new surroundings. I wanted someone to blame, and the new house was something that I could direct my frustration at. My mom and I had to share a room, while my two brothers shared a room. I started at a new school. My dad moved to a motel, and we only got to see him on weekends. Eventually, he moved to a home and again, our whole world felt like it was changing.

I missed my dad, and my siblings and I felt like we had done something wrong to contribute to their divorce. We didn't want our friends to know. It just felt like this GIANT SECRET we couldn't discuss with anyone.

Change can be hard, even if it's for the better, and transitioning to live in two separate homes affected me in ways I didn't expect. My schoolwork was affected, I found it hard to focus, and I lost interest in many things because I was worried about my situation at home. It made me different from everyone else at school, but I didn't talk about it. I just held that feeling inside. I don't even think my teachers knew my situation. Back then in the 1970s, it was taboo to talk about what was going on at home, and divorce was not considered as acceptable as it is today.

My mom raised us the best she could, but she was also hurting. As a newly solo parent, she had to work a lot to pay the bills. Eventually, she met a really great guy and remarried. They bought a home, and we moved into it. We were a blended family: he had four children who also came to live with us. I thought it would be fun to feel like a whole family again but sometimes, it felt like a nightmare. We didn't end up living together long because the jealousy was terrible between us all. To me, he wasn't my dad. I had longed to get my connection back with my biological dad, and my stepfather didn't fill that hole in my heart. He was good to us and provided for us, but it just wasn't the same. Life was totally different and would never be the way it was before.

I didn't talk about how much everything was affecting me. I was so full of anger and sadness and confusion about why this all happened. I missed my dad every day and thought it wasn't supposed to be this way. I even started to blame myself for their divorce. I asked myself over and over what I had done or not done; I felt that if I tried to please people more, I wouldn't get hurt like this ever again. Sometimes we blame ourselves, even if deep down we know it's not our fault.

My parents never really shared with us little kids all the reasons why they had separated. They were trying to protect us from the details because it wasn't about us but not knowing made me feel like I wasn't enough or didn't deserve love. I know now that isn't true, that they had just grown apart and needed to live independent lives to be happy. They were so young when they married, and life had taken different directions for each to follow. It was the best choice for them, but I didn't know how to process all of those big feelings without that information. Not talking about it left me imagining all the ways it was about me but in truth, it had nothing to do with me. My parents still loved me, just from two different places.

I am now sixty-one years old and can now see that opening up about how I felt in those moments would have helped me understand how much I really was loved. I would have learned that sometimes people are just not right for each other, and that's okay. Everything in our lives changes, and while it can feel like it's not for the better, having compassion for what others are going through around us helps to make it easier so that change doesn't always have to be hard.

Three years after my parents separated, my father married the woman he had left my mother for. I was flabbergasted when my soon to be stepmom told me they were getting married. I wish my dad would have told me himself, but I think it was hard for him to explain.

They bought a home in a little village. She had two young girls and to me, they were the perfect kids. They got the childhood I wanted. They stayed home, did plenty of crafts and puzzles, watched movies together with their mom, and had my dad all the time. Sometimes it hurts to see others have what we want. My dad now had a blended family, too, and it felt like they were getting all his time and affection. *"What about your own three kids?"* I would think to myself. I really thought he didn't care, that he was happy with his new life and never knew how much pain I was in. I thought I had lost my dad. All because I didn't know how to express what I was thinking.

I wanted my dad to just say it, to openly tell me, "I love you Karen," but that didn't come naturally to him. It's not how he expressed his love. So I felt like I had to impress him to get his gratitude. I craved for him to say to me, "I'm so proud of you," but those words never came either. He didn't know I needed them, and I always felt like I disappointed him.He didn't know how hard it was to see him give love and affection to what felt like the family that replaced us. I see now how my step-sisters were just much younger than me and that he was doing the best he could to be a good dad in his new surroundings. He didn't mean to make me feel left behind. He wasn't able to read my mind, as much as I wished he could. Telling him how I felt would have helped so much.

I went to my dad's every weekend and met plenty of friends that I still have until this day. But I started to feel like my dad didn't have the right to tell me what to do. It was easier to do what I wanted and deal with the consequences later, but in truth, I was just trying to get his attention. It was my way of receiving some of the love and attention he gave to my younger step-sisters, who I thought were considered little angels compared to me. I was experiencing so many emotions and was just looking for someone to love me and help me understand the pain I was feeling.

Today my dad, now in his eighties, openly tells me he loves me. Our relationship is different from what it was back then. We started to heal when I opened up and shared the words, "I love you."

Today, divorce is looked at differently. It's okay for people to change and grow apart. Sometimes it's the healthiest choice a parent can make. The number of people who go through a separation is openly talked about now; teachers usually know about the situation. Child custody is split in many cases, and it's important to continue talking through the process so that pain doesn't build up or feelings of being unloved don't take over.

If you are going through this in your own family—YOU ARE LOVED. Even if you don't hear the words out loud every day, know that you are loved.

We all carry our pain in different ways. And most times, our family and friends don't know or understand how we feel unless we tell them.

Moving to a new home and school, finding new friends, having new rules, and experiencing step-siblings can be overwhelming, especially when it happens all at once. But things do get better. Sometimes parents don't know that we need them to slow down and take the time to ask us, "How are you feeling with all these changes?" They, too, are often having a hard time and need someone to talk to.

If you feel lonely or like no one understands what you're going through, try writing it down. Let your feelings out and write down your questions. Change affects us all differently; even your pets go through an adjustment period when something changes! Everyone processes it in their own way.

Today, it's okay to share how you're feeling. It's okay to ask for help and gain an understanding of divorce or other big changes. You're not alone. It can be easy to blame one parent or the other when we don't have all the answers; remember, parents don't always know when we are feeling angry or what to do to help when they feel angry, too.

If your family is going through a tough separation, you are not responsible for it. It's not your job to fix it. Remember, families come in all different packages, and love can be found in many different ways.

It feels like just yesterday that my parents told us that my dad was moving out and they were getting a divorce. I remember the words they said, where we sat in the living room, and how I felt at that moment like things were going to change in my life forever. I learned so much about my own emotions through that experience, and it allowed me to see the kind of parent I would like to be when I grew up. I chose to have a house of open communication with my kids, encouraging them to talk to me about anything they were thinking or feeling. We say, "I love you" every chance we get and talk about things that are uncomfortable or challenging to make it easier to experience change.

Do you remember the moment your parents told you they were splitting up or getting a divorce? How did it make you feel? Had you already sensed what your parent(s) were going to tell you? Have you carried this memory with you? Have you ever thought, "If my parents had stayed together, what different path might my life have taken? My education? My marriage? Where would I have gone in life?"

Do your parents split custody? Do you have friends who live with their mom half the week and their other parent half the week? There's no one size fits all. Not one of us experiences divorce the same, not even our brother(s) or sisters(s).

Do you have friends whose parents are still married? Do you feel they are lucky their parents are still together?

Whatever your thoughts and feelings are, they are valid; don't bottle them up.

What happens to us when we are young can sometimes get stuck on replay over and over in our heads. Our experiences make up who we are, but we also need to process and let go of the pain attached to those memories so we don't hold on to them as we grow up. Choosing to focus on happy, joyful, good thoughts helped my mind to heal. Doing so has helped me become the best mom I could be for my kids.

When we focus on the good things that have happened in our life instead of the bad things, our brain starts to put those memories on replay instead. It takes practice and time, but we can all change how we think. Just remember you are not alone. Many of us have been through our parents separating and, in some cases, have gone through our own divorces in adulthood. All I can say is don't dwell on the past. You are a wonderful person, and YOU DESERVE the best life you can have. YOU ARE NUMBER ONE. Look after yourself, be good to yourself, and LOVE YOURSELF.

JOURNAL PROMPTS TO RELEASE ANGER OR SADNESS:

It's important to express our emotions so they don't get stuck or take control of us.

On a piece of paper write, what comes to mind when you read the following questions. (Pen and paper are best instead of the computer, and there's no wrong answers!)

- What makes you feel angry or sad?
- Who do you blame? (Is there someone who makes you feel this way?)
- Why do you blame them?
- Where do you feel this in your body? (The thing you would stay home from school because of: headache, stomach ache, etc. Sometimes our body holds onto emotions if we haven't expressed how we really feel. You might not realize a pain in your body is connected to an emotion that hasn't been released.)
- When does this happen?
- Is there someone you trust who you can share these answers with? When we share our deepest (or hidden) feelings, the people who care about us can better understand how to help.

CHAPTER THIRTEEN

GRATITUDE IS
THE WAY

*"The journey to 'I' is sometimes painful
but so worth finding IT."*

Alma Tarelli

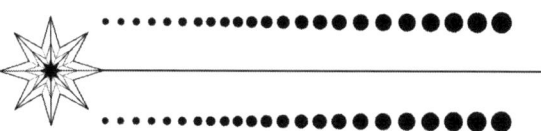

www.AlmaTarelli.com

fb: Alma Tarelli
Goodreads: Alma Tarelli
ig: tarellialma

Alma Tarelli

Alma Tarelli was born and grew up in Albania. She moved to Canada twenty-one years ago.

Having been raised in two extremely different cultures, Alma knows a lot about overcoming trauma and struggles to achieve success in diversity.

Alma graduated university with a degree in business management.Tax accounting is her profession, but being an aspiring wellness guru is her passion. She is committed to raising her three daughters and never stops working and educating herself daily with literature, art, healing, and healthy living.

Alma is passionate about her family, books, yoga, and spirituality. At a very young age, she was an avid reader and developed a love for writing. She has written several essays, poems, and articles in her native language and has been active in writers' social circles in Albania. Alma has also been a keynote speaker at several Women Empowering Events in Vancouver and is winner of several speaking competitions. Her newest passions are yoga and somatic healing. Her goal is to inspire humans to look within and heal themselves.

If not now, when? Alma believes this short journey called life is all worth it!

“ I am grateful for this journey called life!"
"I am grateful for my heart which never skips a beat!"

"I appreciate my mind, body, and soul!"

"I appreciate the beautiful things around me!"

"I appreciate you!"

Can you say these things out loud, at any time? How about when you are having an "it-all-sucks" kind of day? Those lines do sound a bit cheesy, don't they? They might sound down-right cliché to you.

They sounded that way to me. I was not only skeptical; I thought they sounded ridiculous. What was all this hype about gratitude anyway? How can a person "live in gratitude" all the time? To me, this was some Western culture, influenced-by-Oprah kind of thing.

As it turned out, though, Universe/God has always had an answer, a gentle one but one that had to come in its own time. It was up to me to be patient and notice it when it happened.

I was born and raised in Albania. Before the 1990s, Albania was under the Communist regime. Our Communist regime was one of the harshest in Eastern Europe. There was no freedom of speech or choice for how you lived your life. We suffered from extreme poverty, and the Government was God! We were controlled, punished, and destroyed if we opposed the regime. We were excluded from the rest of the world.

My family was intellectual and opposed the regime. For that, we were abused physically, psychologically, and emotionally and discriminated against. All my life, I tried not to talk about my childhood. I locked it inside, never talking about it. In the city where I grew up, people are still fascinated by how we survived.

At the age of seven, I learned how blood smelled when I saw my father covered with it after being attacked by the police. My father was a gentle person who could not speak or hear. He had lost his hearing and ability to talk when he was a child, during World War II. Because of his disability, the government did not put him in jail but rather deported half my family to a concentration camp.

They took my mom and my brother away for three years. I will never forget the crushing pain across my chest as I tried to reach for her arms as they took her. She was crying and trying to keep me to her chest.

Every night, I dreamed of being tucked to sleep by my mother. She used to take my head in her hands, fix my curls, and put my head into her chest. During those years when my mom was away, I wondered and dreamed about her every single night. I longed for so long, crying almost every night, and I could not even pray to God. God did not exist.

They burned my library, saying it had too many "forbidden" books. They did this so people would learn how to obey; the only books people could have were the Communist ideology—Karl Marx and F. Engels.

Seeing *My Little Bear* being burned in the fire was painful.

My whole life growing up was one of all consuming fear. People and friends would not even talk to us. We were called the enemy of the system. We were not to engage with other enemies of the system because we might be complotting against the government.

I had no one left, and I had no idea why my friends would not play or jump rope with me. What does the word "complot" mean anyway?

The main emotions I experienced were constant fear and struggle. Fear of being alone, fear of my family being taken away,- fear of telling the truth, fear of being punished and the fear of police sirens and their possible return to my house. Then there was the sadness and guilt.. The deepest part of me didn't even want to be in this world. Anxiety, inadequacy, and avoidance were the only familiar feelings to me. The word happiness was so foreign to me. We were extremely poor at the time also as the government took away everything, but that was nothing compared to social discrimination, exclusion, and shaming.

"When my mom comes back" was the only thought in my head during those years. My safe place was taken away. I was allowed to visit her in the camp every two weeks for two hours. I never understood why she cried when I would go there and also when I would leave.

"Mama, why do you cry when I come?"

"Because I am happy, Almushka (means little sweet Alma). These are happy tears," she would say.

I would cry only when I was leaving her. Every time I went to visit her, she would ask me what I was reading. "My love," she would say, "you have to read. Read a lot. They can touch our bodies but never our souls." My mom touched my heart with her hand as she said those words.

Books indeed became my escape from reality. I studied hard in school. Even though I was an excellent student, however, I was always disqualified from any competition. I was condemned! Some people would run and look scared if they would hear my last name, while others would have secret mercy in their eyes.

After the 1990s when the regime fell across East Europe, my country opened its borders. But something inside me was shut forever.

I had learned very well how to suppress my emotions.

I continued to read and educate myself. I taught myself English and Italian. This was crucial for my survival. Losing myself in books lets me live in a different reality from my own.

Despite now living in freedom my teenage years were a low self-esteem blob that I compensated for by being a great student. I was kind and very soft in nature yet inside,I was insecure, fearful, and anxious. I did not like it when my friends would talk badly about their parents or their relationship with them. I simply could not comprehend that. To me, the relationship with my mother was the purest form of love. I cherish that connection to this day.

During the Kosovo war in the 1990's, a lot of immigrants came to Albania. I was a student at the time. I served in refugee camps and heard all the traumatic stories. I was fascinated by the way I understood their pain with such ease and made lots of good connections. I became instant friends with a girl my age (nineteen years old). She had lost her brother and her father in the war, and her mother and little brother had crossed the border and immigrated to Albania. She said, "You understand my pain." She went on to say that finding someone who understands your feelings is more important than finding love in this life. I have never forgotten her words.

I studied hard and finished university. My parents were happy. My whole family was happy, as I was the only one who had the chance to go to university.

What more does a weak young girl like me want from life? I had a degree, I started working, and got married.

I thought that finally, the charming prince whom I always had dreamed of would save me from my life. I had read too many fairy-tales. I wasn't even aware of my jealousy, fear of abandonment, and the constant drama that came from my fear of being alone or unloved. My melodramas, tears, and withdrawal that he handled all these years. Poor guy! Actually-a great guy! Even when he would say, "I love you," my mind would ask, "Why would someone love me?" I would roll my eyes in response to any compliment.

I moved with my husband to Canada at the age of twenty-four. Leaving my family was hard, especially my mom.

But this time was different. I deliberately wanted to go. I promised her that I would visit very often. She pretended to believe me.

"When I leave this country, my life will be . . ."

I thought that going away from Albania would make me happy. Forever!

I wasn't! I couldn't escape from myself, No one can,even though I tried.

Being a new immigrant in Canada, struggling socially and linguistically, going through culture shock and being far away from my family again was so hard. I struggled with English in the beginning because of my accent, but I started studying and taking different exams to prove to myself that I could do it. This time was a bit easier for me, because I knew how to cope and survive.

My English was improving somehow but I remained fluent in the habit of melancholy and withdrawal from life, while doing the hard work!

I became a mother of three beautiful children. They taught me how to be a mother. I also got a very good job as an accountant for the government. My family and work was my "happy place," but I was still not happy inside me.

"When we buy this house . . . my life will be happy."

As soon as I bought the dream house, we struggled to pay the mortgage and I became more insecure about the future.

Happiness was a notion that lived in the distant future for me always. "When I do X, then I'll be happy." This was an earworm stuck in me for years.

For me (and I am sure for so many other people), happiness was situational and conditional. It would come after success, achievement, money, status, a certain home, a certain job.

I read many self-help books and I started to realize that we have a happy barometer inside us. When you come from a suffering childhood, your barometer is broken and low. I could not shift the needle of my barometer to get familiar with happiness. Even in the most beautiful moments of my life, (even though at the time, I did not perceive them as such), my mind would say, "Why am I laughing? This feeling is not comfortable!" I would retreat and become withdrawn.

I had a certain pride and momentary satisfaction that came from my achievements, but I was not happy. Happiness is a way of being, not doing. Momentarily satisfaction is not happiness. I also realized that the relationship that we have with ourselves determines the relationship we have with the other main three areas of life: money, relationships and career. I was living in the belief that any of these things can be taken away from you at any time. I tried hard to have them all and still was unfulfilled.

I hit my rock bottom when my mom passed away and I was not able to be there to give her my last goodbye and put my hand on her heart, as she has always done with me. I believe many people in this world are stuck with grief over the death of a loved one, but for me, it was devastating. I felt seven years old again and often would cry in my car so my children would not see me. The pain manifested in my body as heart palpitations and low blood sugar. The grieving process was long, but this time I was determined to ask God/Universe to help me raise my children and have mercy on me.

I needed lots of answers from God. My "why" was urgent!

God took this urgency seriously and started showing me the way. Gently . . .

It took me a decade, but this journey was incredible. I call it my "Journey to I."

I started the loooooooong healing process. During this time, Universe showed me through my work with clients (even though I am an accountant) that I am a compassionate person. I hear others' stories, and I connect easily and deeply. I met people in Canada who grew up orphans and came over as war survivors, and I realized how much suffering there was in the world.

I decided to chase "happy" for the simple reason that I lacked it!

I tried reiki, acupuncture, Traditional Chinese Medicine, EFT, hypno-therapy, Sound healing, inner child work and all kinds of healing modalities that exist. Lots of them. Eating healthy helped a lot in the process. I learned during these years that the low emotion, low self-esteem, body shame, anger, procrastination, stuck-ness, guilt, poor performance, anger and withdrawal, and clinginess we can experience in our relationships stem from trauma experienced in childhood. That trauma stays stuck in your body, particularly in the bones and in the main internal organs.

I also learned that all the negative emotions come from two fears: Fear of being alone and fear of being unloved.

Almost all the self-help books I read brought me to the same conclusions: Live in gratitude and appreciation in the presence. Find a way to make peace with the past and live in the present. After all, the future is not promised to anyone.

I learned that when we are not grateful for the beautiful things that we have, they turn ugly.

I started journaling every single day. I decided to be intentionally grateful daily. It was boring. In the first week, the only gratitude I wrote that felt authentic to me was "I am grateful for my children" or "I am grateful for my family."

I felt I was the most constipated human in history when it came to gratitude. I could not find anything else that I could be grateful for. How can you be grateful when your mind is wired negatively?

But when I start something, I'm committed. After a while, I gradually began noticing daily things that I needed to write down in the evening.

I had so many beautiful things around me. My beautiful children, my family, my house, my work, my career.

I started slowly, very slowly, to find things I could be grateful for daily. On days when I was very sick, I would wake up and say to myself, "I am grateful I woke up today." So many people might not have this privilege.

"I am grateful for this new day." So many people might not be able to see how sunny it is outside.

I walk every day around the lake near my home; when I started my gratitude journey, I started noticing the flowers, the shimmering water where the sun kisses the surface, and the squirrels. Yes, I am grateful for this walk. It seems so small a thing to be grateful for, but it turned out to be a significant signature. The same thing happened with the coffee my husband made for me. Just being polite and saying, "Thank you" is different than truly being grateful and appreciative.

I started getting better at being grateful for things around me. My boss told me that I was the most hard-working person in the office and would take on every task, no matter how difficult. I responded, "I am grateful that you are flexible with me." One week later, she gave me a raise.

This intentional gratitude has some magic inside it. I believe that from the bottom of my heart.

Now becoming grateful for my body and myself—that was enormously hard! I would look in the mirror and see only my flaws: my mommy tummy, my cellulite, my crooked teeth. My eyes would always go to the parts I hated the most, and my mind would agree and laugh her head off at the words, "I am grateful for my body."

Most days, my mind would say, "Who are you kidding, Alma? Don't you see your crooked teeth?"

But then some other days, my mind would be curious.

"Curios" is good!

On those days, I started being specific:

"I am grateful for my heart. It never skips a beat!"

"I am grateful for my back. It has kept me straight for several decades now."

I am grateful for my body; it has kept my heavy head alive for so many years."

I have beautiful, smiley eyes–It took me a long time to really believe this about myself (even though people say it all the time. I have beautiful eyes that they change color when I'm sad.

Self acceptance and self actualization is the only way to find happiness. If you don't think you are pretty enough or good enough, how is someone else going to think that about you?

I started doing yoga daily during this time and have become really good at it. I believe the only way to truly learn something is to be able to teach! So I did exactly that. I took an in-depth yoga teacher training course and started to teach the practice that I am so passionate about. To this day, I am still learning different types of yoga and secrets of ancient healings.

And my feelings about my body were not the only thing to change with gratitude.

"I am grateful for my house." My house started changing and looking more warm and beautiful.

"I am grateful for my husband and the cappuccino he made for me this morning." He felt that! I could smell it in the extra cinnamon he poured in the cup.

Many times, I felt like I was being taken for granted as my family's cook, house cleaner, unpaid math teacher, nurse, etc. So I remind my daughters every evening to express gratitude for the food that I cook and things that I do. And their gratitude is genuine! They appreciate it all. I can feel it in their hugs.

"How does this simple gratitude "thing-y" change everything?" My younger daughter asked.

I smiled and said, "Just try it and you will know the answer!"

My daughters call me GGPS: Gratitude Guru Persona but Sassy.

I laugh; not only do I like it, I embrace it!

Two things that profoundly impacted this journey were the teachings of Louise Hay and Gabor Mate. Louise Hay helped me understand the power of transformation through gratitude Gabor Mate helped me realize that trauma means "both things that happened and things that did not happen for us." Trauma stays in your emotional body for a long time until we decide to release it.

Releasing trauma happens in two ways: up and down in the body.

Up *(mind)* includes mental work like psychology, hypnotherapy, reiki, medication, positive self-talk, positive thinking, affirmations, etc.

Down (body) happens when we move the body with the intention to release. Moving our bones, hips, torso, shoulders, and neck. This is what yoga and breathwork did for me.

Movement of any kind is pivotal in the healing process. Any movement is good: dancing, walking, and playing sports. There is enough medical evidence that shows the importance of physical activity, for the feel good endorphins.

These teachings helped lead me to a few discoveries of my own.

1) When we express gratitude for anything, we learn the other "F" word. "Forgiveness." This word is always in the past tense.

It brings Peace. Peace with the present. Release of the past. This means that we have no resistance and no resentment in our heart. While I can't be grateful for the traumas I had in my life, I am grateful for this journey. Because it is exactly this *human experience that has brought me to my current path.*

2) The moment I say "I am grateful" for an experience and whatever it has taught me, It no longer has a hold on me. Chances are that God will help me let go of it faster if it doesn't serve me any longer.

3) When we are grateful, or even better when we APPRECI-ATE beautiful things in life, God will make sure to give us THAT again or something even better. Appreciation has a golden touch, a finer tune then gratitude. I use appreciation for things I love and admire so God will bless me with more.

During my gratitude journey, I met someone who came close to my heart, a friend who was living life in gratitude. I was mesmerized by the amount of thank-you-s she said during the day, how many times she touched the heart when she spoke, and how she bragged about the little things she accomplished daily. God brought her into my life so I could see first-hand how someone could be just that, even with a horrible story–coming from a broken family, being raised on the streets, and growing up in four different countries. So I ask her "how can someone with that past live a happy life?How can she find sublime simplicity, ease, and fun when the road gets bumpy?Gratitude was the answer! Deep breathing with a hand on your heart.

Maybe you want to argue with me. Maybe you're saying, "Alma, I cannot be grateful for my parents; they were abusive and alcoholic." I agree that it is hard—BUT (sorry for the shouting capitals) parents are humans, too. At one time, they were children and teenagers. They have their own baggage, their own traumas, and they can fail to love us the way we want them to, because they do not love but because they simply CAN'T love us the way we want. They are not capable. Only God will love us the way we want. Our parents are not God! Sometimes parents have a much smaller cup than ours. How can they fill our cup when theirs is a much smaller unit than ours?

Can we be grateful for our imperfect parents? I say YES we can and that we need to. We can be grateful for them, as they are the vehicle that brought us here. Right? God has done a fantastic and astonishing job bringing us here!

We can stay all our life blaming our parents, our circumstances or the world.

The question is: IS it worth it to stay stuck in the victim mentality and then leave this life still waiting for things to change? No one is coming to rescue us!

In the moment when I had enough, I asked God and decided to chase happiness. God opened the doors to me. No more chasing now!

I AM happy and forever grateful for this journey!

All this may sound naive, but I invite you to try it.

Now if you ask me to tell my story again, I would write lots of "I" sentences this way:

I had the privilege of being born and raised in Albania, a diverse country. I experienced the harshest of the regime that made me strong. I had the opportunity to read so many wonderful books and play chess with my father at a very young age. I was blessed as I never doubted or questioned my parents' love for me. "Eat something," "Put the coat on because it is cold outside," or the kiss on the forehead meant love. There was no need for the actual word.

I excelled in math and literature. I finished high school and university with excellent grades. This hunger for education gave me this excellent coping skill and a different view of the world.

I moved to Canada, and it is the best thing that happened to me because this country made me grow and go out of my comfort zone. I live in the most beautiful city in the world.

I married a great guy that handled all my melodramas throughout the years. He is my rock and never fails me! Being supportive, protecting me, and loving me even when I wasn't able to love myself. We healed each other throughout the journey.

Most importantly I am the mother of three wonderful children- this is the absolute greatest privilege one can have in this life. Being a mother, and a parent is the highest title you can have.I get my kids' heads in my hands in the morning as soon as they wake up. I put them in my chest and take a deep breath and smell their hair. There is no other fragrance like that in this life!

I worked as an accountant for the government in Canada, and it has opened so many doors for me. I still work as a Tax specialist for a wonderful office, where I find fresh flowers daily from my clients.

I live an embodied life as a healer, a yoga teacher, and so many other things that my soul wants to experience—and it's still downloading.

I am proof of a great and successful life. My soul is still wanting to experience more. This life is way too short and fantastic not to take this opportunity and be grateful daily.

"I am a prosperous, beautiful, and powerful soul."

And if that past version of me—scared and fearful and not enough and without a voice and fragile and skinny like a skeleton—made it, I guarantee you ANYONE can make it!!!

Trust your journey, no matter how difficult it looks. Trust God–as you are in good hands.

I wish there was a subject in school called Grati-study, the science of gratitude. But nevertheless we are all in a school called "life" and we are tested daily. So breathe and be grateful for this breath—the most precious thing in life and the closest thing to us. Tomorrow morning, someone might not have this privilege of breathing.

It is my wish that everyone comes to live in gratitude for the little things in life . I am grateful for you, for reading this! I APPRECIATE you!

Tell me, what are you grateful for today? Are you able to rewrite your life story up to this moment from a lens of gratitude and appreciation?

CHAPTER FOURTEEN

EXOTIC COWS, AND LIFE.

"You got time kid."

Ruth Lorraine Brown

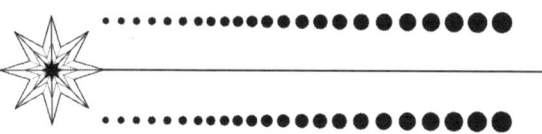

Fb: ruth.ibbotsonschell
Ig: redchild65
Tiktok: ruthibbotsonbrown

Ruth Lorraine Brown

Ruth Brown is originally from Kluskus First nations in Quesnel BC, but calls Three Hills Alberta her home. She's on a path to finding out who she is and to advocate for Indigenous rights. Ruth is on a quest to be less quirky, and learn how to deal with her ADHD. She's a wife and mom and the friend you'd call to help bury a body. She's here to let people know that it's never too late to figure your life out.

I was a quirky kid . . . with a big nose and big glasses. One day, I decided to get a perm because back in the late '80s, spiral perms were a big thing. *Full House* was the show of the moment, so tiny blonde girls with blue eyes and the perfect curls were the gold standard for beauty. So when this gawky Indigenous girl with long, thick hair got a perm from the small-town way-past-middle-aged hairstylist that my mom, grandma and aunt all went to...it was a disaster. The frizz was unbelievable. I thought that the brush was my friend, but it betrayed me.

During that time, our grade five class was studying indigenous cultures and my teacher asked me to do a presentation to the class on the tribe I was from. I knew the name of the tribe but since I was adopted as a baby into a white evangelical Christian family, I really had no clue about the indigenous culture and had to research from a book. I remember being so embarrassed and ashamed because I was so different from my classmates- all I wanted to do was fit in and be like everyone else. I decided that day: my plan when I was older was to dye my hair blonde, tell everyone I was from California and maybe people would think that the color of my skin was a beautiful beach tan.

In 1995, Disney came out with *Pocahontas* and I fit the bill. I had finally figured out makeup and knew now to stay away from perms. My culture was popular, and I didn't care if it was a passing fad. I still had no clue who I was but was eager to please everyone around me- and was happy to play the role of Disney princess while it was still popular. I was also eager to please my conservative Christian community; my faith had taught me to never question authority, to not rock the boat, and to think and operate inside the box. What people thought about me mattered. This started an internal struggle: who I was, including my newfound interest in my culture and my unique self, didn't line up with what my religion expected of me. I was expected to study theology, be sweet and submissive, and get married. (Bonus points if I could be a missionary to another culture and save them from eternity in hell. All they needed to do was reject everything they knew, accept our God and start wearing pleated pants and a polo top and they would be saved from an eternity in hell). At that point, my interest in my own culture was for me to go back to my people and to share my faith, in hopes they would turn from their pagan beliefs and give their heart to Jesus Christ. I hadn't really started to get to know myself or to celebrate and embrace my culture, my family, and my connection to generations of ancestors. To do this would be to reject the one and only way to achieve salvation and live a dedicated Christian life.

So I left town and joined the military. It was the only way I could see avoiding an early marriage, popping out kids and working as a cashier at the grocery store for the rest of my life–because that's what you do in my small town. I went on an adventure to figure myself out and stretch my limits but all I was really doing was escaping what was expected of me. I would need to spend the next twenty years finding out who I was and what I was capable of. I had to find out what my true culture was and when I did, I started loving it. I was able to shed old ideas of what faith and religion were and to find a life I was happy to live. I began working through trauma from my adoption, which included abandonment issues from my biological mother, generational trauma from the residential school system and biological parents that suffered from addiction and trauma from horrific abuse.

Here's what I learned and how I learned it: it's never too late to figure out who you are and what you need to heal from. I always thought I was a scatter-brained laid back low-energy procrastinator. However, some of these traits are actually a trauma response passed on from my biological parents who went through the residential school system. That horrific experience both of them had growing up created a series of events that has affected my whole family, including my adopted family. They both did what they could to heal but had a lifelong struggle with alcohol abuse. My biological mother had me at sixteen and had no tools to process the abuse she suffered during her childhood. She was taken from her mother, who was taken from her mother. So when she found out she was pregnant with me, she didn't feel capable of raising a baby. While pregnant with me, she was dealing with her own trauma and passed trauma on to me. As a result, my body responded by going into fight-or-flight and shutdown mode. Understanding this made sense of my reactions and let me be easy on myself when I needed to be and to push when I needed to push. I also started researching how to recover from this: what things I needed to do like meditate, breathwork, therapy, and nutrition.

I was diagnosed with ADHD as an adult which also explained the complete lack of doing anything efficiently! My greatest wish is to be competent, focused and efficient . . . yet here we are. My greatest strength is wasting valuable time researching exotic cow breeds, volcanic patterns throughout the world and how to sign swear words in American Sign Language. Don't get me wrong-these are all fascinating topics and might come in handy if I ever own a sassy deaf highland cow in Bali. However my current life in rural Alberta would benefit more if I could manage money, use my time wisely, pull the trigger on starting my company, get some more education and finish writing my autobiography. Fortunately, the more I learn about ADHD the more I find help (eg. life-hacks, nutrition, medication) for people who struggle with this. Also, it takes all kinds of people for the world to function. I've got personality, spunk and charisma. I am a people person. I am empathetic and caring. This will take you far if you know where to direct your talents and personality.

I also started connecting with my indigenous culture in my late thirties. I met up with my biological family whenever I could to connect, love, and learn. One of my best friends in life is my brother, Geronimo. He has taught me indigenous ceremonies and told me stories about my parents and grandparents. I never thought my little brother would be my teacher and mentor! He even performed a traditional marriage ceremony (that he learned from my grandpa) for me and my husband. We rented a helicopter and got married on the top of a mountain-the way my ancestors have done it for thousands of years. It was one of the most important moments of my life that I got to share with my husband, Geronimo and my sister.

The marriage ceremony experience connected me to my grandfather and every other ancestor throughout time. I waited to connect because I was scared and insecure about what my family would think about me. I realized being scared was something I could push through and that I loved my family and worrying about what they thought of me was counter-productive to my goal. Besides, I'm still a bit quirky: I was raised by white people and am still trying to fit in on the Rez! They have to cut me some slack knowing all that! My family has been amazing at loving and accepting me. My adoptive family has also been amazing at supporting me and providing a safe and loving home for me to grow up. I have amazing brothers and sisters on both sides of my family. I couldn't have done all this without love and support from my adoptive parents and my husband. This gave me the ability and space to focus on healing. I felt that in my thirties after a failed marriage, I needed to address those issues. I started counseling with a really good doctor who introduced me to some really great authors. I started to read books and listen to podcasts focused on emotional healing, health and nutrition, psychology and neuroscience. I started following my favorites on YouTube, Tiktok and whatever social media they might use. Some highlights include *The Four Agreements* by Don Miguel Ruiz, *Power vs Force* by Dr David R. Hawkins, *The Untethered Soul* by Michael A. Singer, anything by Louise Hay, Ryan Holiday, Robert Greene and all books by Dr Gabor Mate. I listen to Dr. Rhonda Patrick *Found my Fitness* Podcast, Dr Andrew Huberman Huberman *Lab Podcast*, Dr. Zubin Damania *The ZDogg MD Show Podcast*.

I am a work in progress. I started a bit late- but it's never too late to figure this stuff out. It's a journey that will never end and will continue on with my kids. I'm finally living a life where I understand who I am, why I am the way I am and to care for myself and appreciate what I've done and what I can offer those around me. I can look back and laugh at myself and look forward to providing a great future for myself and my family. I've grabbed tools and support along the way–and most importantly I've figured out that the hair straightener is my best friend!

How to Embrace
Your Greatest Strength

1) What makes you quirky or different from others?

2) What parts of your culture do you love the most?

3) What hidden talents do you have?

4) What is your greatest strength?

Complete the following phrase to create a powerful affirmation:

I am:

ACKNOWLEDGMENTS

Thank you, my children, for the wisdom, awareness, healing, laughter, and magic you continue to bring to my life. I am deeply grateful you chose me to be your mum. Love you forever.

-Stephanie Burgess

To all the brave survivors of childhood victimization. Acknowledging a personal history of abuse takes enormous courage. The abuse you suffered is not who you are; it's what happened to you. You are not alone.

-Leslie Anne Hook

To everyone who believed in me when I didn't believe in myself—I love you all so very much! Thank you, Mom, for handing me my fork. You are my hero!

-Heather Marie Spitzer

To my inner child who thought she needed to be what everyone else expected of her, thank you for being brave and following your dreams to uncover your own magic that was hiding.

-Kady Romagnuolo

For my daughters, Marina, Catalina, Charlotte, and Sophie. May you know that, in my eyes, you will always be perfect.

-Mary FR Smith

Thank you to my children who have given me the opportunity to do things differently. You have helped me grow into the mentor I needed as a child.

-Karen Brunette

To my mother, the deepest appreciation for her unconditional love, strength, wisdom and grace. And to my father, whose strength through his pain and adversity will continue to give me courage and hope.

-Leah Marie Scott

My son Callan has deeply expanded my worldview and inner awareness, and I am forever grateful for him. I would also like to thank my parents, husband, and Kady for their inspiration and unwavering belief in me.

-Marisa Brona O'Brien

I dedicate this chapter to Jacob Small, a brave thirteen-year-old at the time this chapter was written. You are a natural born Hero and an Emerging Leader.

-Naomi N. Ali

Thank you, my children, for the wisdom, awareness, healing, laughter, and magic you continue to bring to my life. I am deeply grateful you chose me to be your mum. Love you forever.

-Ruth Fae

To my Husband, daughter, and family. To Ernie, Laura and Kelley. They helped change my life for the better. I'm forever grateful.

-Karla Torres

My loves Thankyou for teaching me how to be a mother. It's my absolute privilege to have you in this life. I am forever grateful to God that gifted me the three precious you!

-Alma Tarelli

My deepest gratitude to my parents for their love and for providing a safe environment where I can thrive and grow. To Paul. I love you, thank you for believing in me.

-Ruth Lorraine Brown